Louise

Anna Decormier

Louise
All Rights Reserved.
Copyright © 2022 Anna Decormier
v1.0

This is a work of fiction. Names, characters, businesses, places, events, locales, and incidents are either the products of the author's imagination or used in a fictitious manner. Any resemblance to actual persons, living or dead, or actual events is purely coincidental.

The opinions expressed in this manuscript are solely the opinions of the author and do not represent the opinions or thoughts of the publisher. The author has represented and warranted full ownership and/or legal right to publish all the materials in this book.

This book may not be reproduced, transmitted, or stored in whole or in part by any means, including graphic, electronic, or mechanical without the express written consent of the publisher except in the case of brief quotations embodied in critical articles and reviews.

Outskirts Press, Inc.
http://www.outskirtspress.com

ISBN: 978-1-9772-5374-3

Cover Photo © 2022 www.gettyimages.com. All rights reserved - used with permission.

Outskirts Press and the "OP" logo are trademarks belonging to Outskirts Press, Inc.

PRINTED IN THE UNITED STATES OF AMERICA

Dedication page

*I wish to thank
Robert McGee
1932-2013*

For without his enthusiasm this book would not have been written

The Woman

She was a long, black, curly haired, brown-eyed young beauty. To tell you how she got here would be a whole other story. Her mother and father, who were lost to her, gave her name to her. Louise, a very simple name for a young woman who is about to take a step into mystery and madness.

It was cold, very cold, and she was tired and filled with fear. She was alone, really alone for the first time in her life. She had just turned 18 two days ago. Then she had been filled with great expectation of a train journey out west. Now there was darkness, fear, cold and sounds she did not know.

As she walked through the tall trees, she heard a sound in front of her that only brought compassion to her heart. It sounded like a whimper filled with pain and fear. About twenty-five feet in front of her, lying in the bushes was a white wolf. He was hurt. She could see the blood all down his side. He saw her and bared his teeth and made a guttural sound from within.

Long after she would wonder why she did not feel fear; only compassion, as if he was hers to care for. She realized they were very near water; she could hear it. It couldn't be far. She reached down and tore a piece of her petticoat off and went in search of the water. Over a small hill to the left of the wolf there was a stream. She wet her petticoat and returned and stood about four feet from the most beautiful beast she had ever seen. His fur was like snow with small specks of glitter. His head was held high even in pain and fear. His body shook. His eyes met hers and something touched her soul. He nipped at her all the time she cleaned him until she found the bullet wound. The bullet had gone all the way through. She cleaned the wound and dressed it with the torn piece of her petticoat. She sat close enough to keep him warm until they fell asleep.

When she awoke the sun felt good on her face and for a moment she forgot where she was. But then she remembered the feeling of lying close to the warm body of the beast. She opened her eyes and with joy and sadness saw he was gone. Joy because he stood off in the distance as if he had never been shot, sadness because she missed his closeness. But she had the feeling of family just by seeing him. Something of her felt different as if she had touched or seen her own soul in this animal.

After washing at the stream, she found berries to eat and prayed that God would lead her on her journey; where ever that may be.

It was getting late in the day and now the big problem would be a place to spend the night. Up the hill and by the stream there seemed to be a place were the earth hung over as to make a small cliff. Under there with dry leaves maybe sleep would come. A voice startled her. When she turned, only the wolf was there by the stream watching. She was not sure when he joined her in the night. She remembered only the warmth he brought with him and in the morning the only sign he had been at her side was a small amount of white hair on what was left of her petticoat.

The next animal encounter came about midmorning at the stream; she was in the water trying to catch a fish. Something that, bare handed, was, to say the least, impossible. Then a bear approached the stream. Once again, she felt no fear, just wonder. If this was her end, what a magnificent creature to end it; but, his eyes like the wolf's, met her only with knowing. He threw her a fish and left.

In her heart she knew something was different about her. Almost like someone else was with her. When she lifted her head, she saw about 50 feet up stream what seemed to be a cabin that the wilderness had taken over. Maybe a place to rest and try to understand what was happening to her. She walked slowly toward the cabin.

The Man

He, among his people, was the young chieftain to be; strong in body and knowing in the old ways. He was one with nature. He had killed White man and he felt only power. Who were these people? They only killed and wasted nature; they were not one with the Earth. They only ruined all that they touched. But yesterday he saw White with nature. He saw the beauty of body and soul. A woman: a White woman, alone in the woods, one who got away from the killing on the train. One he followed and was about to take when she went to the wolf. The white wolf: the symbol of nature itself, sleeping with her, watching her, guarding her. It was against all he knew. A woman! A White woman!

He remembered after following her from the train that she rested at the old burial ground. She seemed to not know what was happening to her. He had planned to follow her and let the wilderness kill her. He could tell by just watching her she was young and did not have any idea of how to survive on her own. But she made him yearn to know her. Her body was not like an Indian woman. She was large breasted and small waisted and her hips were for child bearing. He did not understand why he desired her. He could not keep his eyes off her or keep from wondering what she was or had become.

He was born to lead his people. He had learned all about how to be one with nature. It hadn't been easy. He had gone through all the trials, all the tests; never doubting anything taught him. But he had never saw a white wolf, let alone one sleeping with a human and at that a White woman.

He needed to speak to the learned ones; he must take the story to them. They would know what to do. He would tell them about the mist that came around her at the burial ground, how he felt the spirit of the old one nearby. He must tell them of the wolf and bear that now followed her.

He remembered the old story that told of the old one, the great sprit coming back to lead his people from harm, and to bring knowledge of the future. The legend said he would join with a being to bring a great leader, one to bring the white and the Indian together. One to help them in times of trouble. And this was a time of trouble, the white man had come with his iron horse to kill and destroy the land. His people suffered. They had taken their food, the buffalo and their land, killed their women and children and even tried to call them friends. Now would be the right time. But it could not be a woman, maybe a young chief, but not a woman. He must go to the camp, but it was hard to leave the woman. She had gone to the old cabin and the wolf and bear were with her watching outside and, high above, an eagle soared. He must get to the learned ones. They would know what to do. They had told of the coming of the sprit for generations passed down from one chief to the next. Could this be what they were waiting for? Or did this woman ruin any chance of the legend coming true.

The White man was coming closer and closer with their iron horses and guns. He could see there wasn't much time before they would be pushed into the mountains and then left to die in the winter. There were just too many of them, but he would not stop hunting them until he died. They came and said they were friends and then burned and killed. These people knew nothing about the way of the spirit; only of their greed and want.

    If the spirit had joined with this woman, she must not be able to leave this land. She would have to be kept here or the learned ones, maybe, can have the spirit go to another and then he could kill her. But his mind told him he could not harm her. He was having trouble just leaving her; how could he kill her?

The Cabin

Louise approached the cabin. Something inside her felt that this was to be her home. She was just 18. How did she make a home; she remembered the sweet smells & laughter and love (lots of love) of her home. Her mother and father loved her and made her happy and safe all these 18 years. She thought her life was well planned out. A good marriage: a wonderful husband with lot of kids and many happy hours with her family. Her family, were they all dead. Was she the only one who got away? Why did they do this to them?

As she closed her eyes, she felt like the past was another person's life. What had happened? How did she get here? Who was she? Something inside her had changed when she rested by that place. It was a very different place then she had ever seen before but she was so tired she had to lie down. It had high tables with stuff she had never seen before hanging from them and she was sure there were skeletons on the tables. She remembered she felt frightened at first but then a feeling of peace overtook her. She fell into a deep quiet sleep. When she woke up, she felt like she was a different person.

But right know she must go on with trying to make a place to rest and feel safe. Safe, she did feel safe, like she belonged here. The wolf, the bear and all the animals felt like family, her new family.

They stayed very close and she had no fear of them. Something had made her realize they were part of her; but, what part. I am she thought, just a child of 18, I do not understand all this, but the feeling of being safe was good enough for now.

The cabin was old. It was built on the side of a cliff. It almost couldn't be seen from the stream. The woods had tried to overtake it and had almost succeeded. The roof was part of the cliff and the rest of it was large logs and mud put together to keep the weather out. It had one small door and a very little window. There was only one way in and out that could be seen. That could be good and bad. No one could get in the back because it was part of the hill but then you couldn't get out the back either. Maybe there could be a way out the back that wasn't easy to see. If the person that built it was smart, there would be a back way out. After seeing what happened at the train to her and her family, she wondered what happened to the people who lived here before.

She looked again at the one door and window and it warmed her heart. The steps were almost rotted out and the door hung to one side and the window was open. She laughed!! Open to life. The small piece of glass was not broken. Maybe the people just had left after all and there was no bad thing that had happened here. Maybe it could be a safe place for her to stay until she could make sense out of what had happened. She pushed the door to the side and entered.

It was cold. The earthen floor and one wall made it cool even in the sun. She saw a pit for fire. As she looked around the room she saw one chair, one small round table and a coffee pot. Over on a small shelf there was one plate and a cup. Just enough, she was alone after all. Then she saw who must have built the cabin, only bones now. The arrow seemed to have hit his heart. So, this place wasn't untouched by the hate. She didn't have a choice to go somewhere else this was it.

It didn't take her long to dig a grave. It was spring and the ground was soft. She put the man to rest. She prayed he would find the peace that she felt. Funny all this and she felt at peace. Something was different about her. She didn't know what, but it was nice and she didn't want to question it. For now, she would be at peace.

As she was returning to the cabin, she gathered wood. Maybe she could start a fire and stay warm tonight. By the pit there was flint to start the fire. Funny, she felt very happy making this place home. Why? At first, she didn't notice there was food at the door, a piece of a small animal and a fish. She looked all around to see if her new friends (the Wolf, Bear and Eagle) were around. She could not see them but knew they were close. She could feel them watching her and feel their warmth. She had no fear of them; just great joy. Next, was getting some water. She only had a small cup and a bowl but the stream was close and she didn't need much.

She spent hours cleaning and straightening up the cabin, making a bed from leaves, setting up her little table and bringing water in from the stream. It was getting dark and she felt very tired. She lay on the bed looking out the little window wondering where her real home was. She knew it was lost to her but if she could remember maybe she would be able to put it to rest. Not knowing what happened to her family nagged at her. She could smell the fire and feel the warmth. She felt safe and at peace. And she knew whatever was in front of her was past her ability to change.

It felt like someone was with her. She seemed to know more about the place and the animals then she should. There was a feeling of something to come, a new beginning and great joy. As she looked at the stars, she felt a presence in her, she new it was a spirit of something good and wise, with a great need that seemed to be greater than she could understand. Part of her knew that she didn't have to understand, just do what was asked of her. Maybe the dreams she couldn't remember from her past would be replaced by a promise coming true. A promise made to many for a long time. Maybe it would hold a better future than she would have had and maybe not. It didn't matter; she knew it had to be.

When sleep came her dreams were filled with sights and sounds new to part of her and familiar to another part.

The Wolf joined her in the middle of the night and the bear stood watch.

The Spirit

He wasn't sure how many old wise ones were part of him, only that he held all the knowledge of the past. He was here to bring a leader. Someone to lead his people not, to fight, but to be among the white as an equal. The people have waited for a long time for a leader, but the leader he was to bring was not what they had expected. He would grow up as a white and bring the knowledge back to his people. He would join with the child to be. He was with his mother now. She was a strong white woman. He wasn't sure of all the feelings in her but he was sure about her. When he saw her rest by the burial ground, he knew she was the vessel of the future. He must protect her and keep her safe. She was to be the mother of the future.

He believed in the goodness of man but knew the strength of an idea. He must take the strength and goodness in the young chief and mix it with the beauty of the soul and heart of Louise. She was the key. He was the teacher.

His people had called for many years for help. He had heard them but the time was not right. He knew their sorrow and fear and wished he could give them their peace. He couldn't; he must take all the steps that were known to him from the years of knowledge. They must be able to be among the whites to survive. Their strength and heritage would only make them better people, but the hatred and fear must be taken out of their hearts. The only way was to give them a leader, one who had knowledge of both (White and Indian) and who would lead them to their place in the new world to come.

The learned ones at the camp already knew she was here. They knew he was with the White woman. The legend talked of the mother of the future. They told of her not being of their world. They told of her inner strength and her willingness to give all to what was her destiny. They told of her beauty of flesh and soul. All the animals knew when they looked into her eyes that the spirit of man and animal was part of her. Soon he would teach her how to use all the knowledge he possessed. She would be an easy student. He could feel her mind reaching for his knowledge already. She wanted to know her future and wanted to know all the knowledge she could to complete her future with honor and strength.

If he was a young buck again, he would want her. She was so perfect in every way. Her face was that of a young angel. Her brown eyes were large and sparkled like glitter. Her skin was flawless, almost pure white, but her checks held a small pocket of rosy red. Her lips were full and red in color. And then there was her smile: it was like a flash of warmth. Her tears were like diamonds on snow. He loved her and he would bring the magical change and would help her on her journey to be the mother of their future.

But first he must teach her how to survive. She would spend a large amount of time on her own. The animals and learned ones would make sure of her survival. The animals would protect her and the learned ones would let everyone know who she was and all would help her.

He must teach her from within. He must teach her to face fear and to embrace the future. He needed to fill her mind with the way of the red man, and she needed to know all the Indian ways so she could teach the child to be. He needed to teach her all the legends and all the history before the child was born. Even though the child had not been conceived time was short. The young chief wouldn't even know what drove him to her but he would come to take her and bring his seed to be the future of his people. The learned ones would tell him his part. They would purify him and pray over him for two weeks, and then he would come for her. He would be dressed as a tribal chief but he would carry a relic of all the chiefs of his tribes with him. He would bring them honor and a future for his nation.

He felt that he would also love her, for she filled him with love. Maybe it was her goodness and beauty or just the feeling of knowing she was the one to help his people make it in the new world that was coming to them very soon. He had waited for centuries for this and it seemed such a short time now. He hoped he would bring the legend to pass; he hoped he had the strength to give her to someone else.

He was one with her, he could feel her breath and he knew her hopes and fears. She dreamed of the child she was to have and her heart was so full of joy he felt like his soul was about to burst. He felt his arms were wrapped around her and he could feel her head on his chest, smell the sweet scent of her hair and feel the soft skin touch his. Yes, he did love her but he had a mission from long ago to follow and must remember that.

In knowing her he understood a mother's love and knew why this woman must be with the boy. Her love would overcome all the hate and fear in his people... she would teach the boy to love and he would learn to love before he learned to feel anger or hate. He would be a great leader; he would become the mother and father of his people, the love and strength all in one.

This woman, this White woman, was all their future and he loved her and he hoped after she understood she would love him too. At this moment he wished he was to be the instrument that would bring her the child. He yearned to touch her flesh but he knew he was only the knowledge and was happy to at least be able to know her. He had waited through centuries of apprenticing to pass on the knowledge. He wouldn't have believed all the joy and love she brought him, a spirit of many. All the past loved her and the future would too. He was sure of the future now and he new it would be like all the legends said. His people would be saved by a White woman.

The Wolf slept with her and kept her warm; they must get her the right clothes and blankets. She must have the right food to keep her healthy.

Tomorrow he would send the animals to the camp for clothing and blankets, the learned ones would know why they had come and would be ready.

The Camp

He heard the drums even before he realized what they were. He had just left the woman while she slept. He had looked into the window and the Wolf slept close to her. The Wolf lifted its head and looked at him. He could sense that he belonged there. The Wolf lay back down beside her as if he wasn't an intruder. She lay on her side. Her face reminded him of the old stories of the beautiful spirits. This was surly what they would have looked like.

He could sense the presence of the spirit world. He thought maybe this was only a dream, but part of him knew better. There was a great yearning in him that he didn't understand. He felt his thoughts and deeds to come would not be his, but that the spirits had taken over his destiny.

He wished he could touch her, just lay his hand on her face. His breath became labored like he had run a long way, his chest felt full and about to burst. He must leave or he wouldn't be able to. The Wolf rose as if reading his thoughts. He turned and left.

Even as he was running for the camp, he couldn't get the picture of her lying there out of his mind. He was a young man in all ways but he had never longed just to be with a woman. They had their purpose. They were to take care of a man's pleasure and have his children; this was a great part in the cycle of life. They were to be respected but only yearned for when nature made the man want her body. This he understood. He did not understand how he felt about this White woman. Yes, he wanted her but not just for the moment. He wanted to make her want him, to make her smile at him, to give her joy, to understand what made her, her.

He could hear the drums getting louder and louder. They seemed to be coming from in his head, and he knew this was the beginning of his journey into a legend. It was as if he was watching from the outside of his body.

The drums were so loud now they hurt his head. He closed his eyes and when he opened them up, he was in the purifying tent. The tent was a circle about 8 feet in diameter. In the middle a fire kept rocks hot and water was poured over them to make steam. He was sitting in a circle with all the learned ones (the Whites called them witch doctors). He was naked and almost in a dream state. He heard them praying to the great spirit for the legend to begin.

He saw himself running with the Wolf, flying with the Eagle and sleeping with the Bear. He was one with nature; so much knowledge rushed into his brain. The entire past of his race and the promise of the future. He knew he was the one to bring the seed of his people. He felt pride and joy. He knew the woman would bear a boy child, the one to lead his people. He knew his part but he wanted more; he wanted her to be his. Why couldn't they both raise the boy? He was a warrior. He would be the better teacher of the Indian ways. He could teach the boy all about nature and survival. Why must he give her up? He was to be chief and with her by his side he could help bring the legend to the present. He could lead his people to win over the White man. Why must he give her up?

He seemed to see the future in a daze. Many Red and White men dying. Many promises made and broken. How could the boy change this? Was he to be a great warrior, one to lead them to defeating the white man? Something inside him said no. He was going to bring knowledge and leadership to walk with the White man. This was a concept he did not understand. How could they trust them let alone walk with them? He felt confused. He prayed the spirits would enlighten him.

His dream state became deeper. He saw the woman with the boy. He knew the sprit of the old ones were with the boy. He saw the young one grow in body and in knowledge. He saw him learn all the white and red man's ways. He now understood that after he grew to manhood, he would return to lead his people. He would take his father's place as chief and lead his people in a world his father could not understand. A world where Red and White walked together to bring about a good life for both, where both, remembered and forgave.

He could feel the heat and hear the learned one's prayers. How he wanted her. He could feel her flesh hot and full. He almost felt crazy. He knew that some of the craziness was from the spirits and some from him wanting her and not wanting to give her up.

He would take her and give her the seed of the future and he would take her as his. He was chief and he would bring her and the child to his tent and they would all be one. The tribe would believe in him and would follow him. He would convince the learned ones he was with the spirit and they would help him. He must have her and keep her. His desire for her was more than he could contain.

He must have been in this dream state for weeks. When he awoke all his strength was gone. They brought him food and drink and he slept a sound, deep sleep. One that would fill him with strength to fulfill his density.

Louise

She had spent many days just looking around. Blankets, clothing (all Indian), fire wood, all kinds of food were left day after day at her door. They must come at night when she slept. She never saw anyone but knew she was being watched.

Day after day her knowledge of the Indian ways and the ways of nature become like she had learned them from a child. She knew that this knowledge came from within. She felt it was good but it also frightened her.

She had very limited memory of her past, but she did believe in God and her greatest fear was this teacher in her was not from God. The only thing that made her feel it was good was the animals. When they were with her, they were gentle and loving creatures; surely, only good men would make them so.

The Wolf stayed with her day and night. The Bear slept at her door, the Eagle watched from the tree, what a wonder all this was. What a blessing to see these wonders of nature so close. She must be dreaming or maybe she died at the train and she was in heaven, maybe, maybe.

She dreamed every night about a child, an Indian child dressed as White. She felt great joy in this dream but wasn't sure what it could mean for her.

She felt the spirit in her was a man. His thoughts were sometimes what seemed to be those of a lover. When she slept, she felt his body beside her and the Wolf. She somehow knew he was getting to be a part of her and at the same time new he would leave and she would miss him.

She didn't know much about love; she was a young girl. She knew she had sensations that she never had before.

When she was in deep thought she longed to be held and touched. She wanted to feel the pleasure of giving and receiving to a man. The only problem was the one she loved was a spirit. What she knew of the future was his teaching. She knew there was a man and knew it wasn't the spirit. How could he give her to someone else? How could this be?

She was startled by the Wolf. He stood and growled. Men approached.

There were two men, one her age, one older. They rode horses and wore buck skin coats. They must be trappers. She saw animal skins on their horses. They had guns. She saw them look at the wolf and she feared they may shoot him. She sent him away.

The younger man said, "You must be the woman that all the Indian tribes are talking about. They say you walk with the animals but if I hadn't seen it, I wouldn't have believed it. They say you're the mother of the future. I don't understand; you're White."

She listened to all he said. She was to be the mother of the future. She was to mate with the young chief and their child (the boy in her dreams) would lead the Indians to peace. Now she understood why the boy dressed as White. She still wished it could be the spirit within her. But she should make her guests at home.

The older one was the younger one's father. He was frightened for her and felt he and his son should take her from here. He sensed that she was a part of a plan and he, as a father, should save her. She didn't seem afraid.

She made them dinner and talked to them about all the wonderful things that had happened to her. He sensed she didn't remember the past. He was about to tell her when she told them she remembered a train ride but only saw the rest of her past as someone else's life. She felt she had family and a life somewhere else before but it all seemed like a dream. She did know her name was Louise, but didn't know her last name. She remembered pretty dresses and nice smells; it made her smile. The young man couldn't take his eyes off her smile.

The old man didn't tell her the train was attacked by Indians. He felt she must still be in shock because something was very strange about her. She almost seemed like two people. One a young beautiful girl and the other a knowing woman who has seen centuries of life and remembered it all. Maybe there was a spirit from the graves not too far from there. He had trapped this area for years and knew the legend about what was to come. Could this be what was happening with this young girl? Was she the one the drums were talking about? They had heard them for days, louder and louder. He felt old. Part of him was like a father and wanted to get her out of here and the other part was in awe of what might be happening. They must be careful or they could be like the trapper who had owned the cabin they were now in. He had removed relics from the graves and now was dead.

His son could only see her beauty and he was sure if the boy ever touched her, they would both die. They must be very careful. His son felt she was the most beautiful woman he had ever seen. She was like an angel. He could watch her move all night and when she talked it was like she sang. He knew his father and he must get her out of here, but how? The Indians were all around. He felt they had let them get here, but why? Maybe they thought she needed her own kind to talk to. It didn't matter but she did. She must be saved and he would talk to his dad and they would come up with a plan. She belonged with her kind, her family and, maybe, someday him.

They spent the rest of the evening talking about her and what had happened in the last two weeks. They were spell bound by the animals that she called family. They also could sense she had no fear of what was coming, only great expectations of joy.

After about two hours of talk the old man knew she was possessed by a spirit. He was not an Indian but had seen the working of their great respect for their ancestors. He realized the spirit had made her accept her destiny. They must help her, but how.

He watched his son become more and more in love with her and his fear grew to great heights.

The sun was going down and they must leave the cabin, they would camp by the stream. The Wolf came in the window and lay at her feet. It was time to go.

At the stream they talked about getting her out of this place. They would have to go for help. There was a group of about 100 soldiers camped by the train. They must go back and get them to help. They were looking for the governor's daughter. He didn't know her name but it must be this girl. She matched the description. How would her father feel when he found out his daughter was possessed with an Indian spirit?

The father and son were asked by the governor to look for her. As trappers they could get through. He, years before, was a scout for the army and his son was now. He had a feeling they were part of the legend or they wouldn't have got to her at all. It frightened him and he had never felt this kind of fear before.

He could see her through the open door. The Wolf lay on her hip and the Bear lay across the front door, protection all around. No one or thing would harm her. Even though he felt for her, he was glad he could witness this oneness with nature. Dear God help her and us.

In the cabin Louise's mind filled with thoughts that bothered her. These men made her want to remember the past but something inside her would not allow it. Was it that the spirit wanted her and feared she would leave if she knew all? Surly he must feel her great love for him. She couldn't bear to be without him, and life would end if he was gone. She would only he half full; she dreamed he held her. She could feel his strong body lay beside her. She had never known a man but she wanted him to know her body and her to know his body. The dream was full of love and wonderful wants fulfilled.

The spirit couldn't stay loving her in her dreams. He knew it wasn't supposed to be this with her. But he never had felt such drive to be close to someone before. When she smiled at the young man, he could have killed him. How was he supposed to give her to the young chief? It had to happen but for now he would make love to her, if only in her dreams.

In the morning she fed her two new friends and with tears in her eyes said goodbye. The young man kissed her cheek and she felt her breath in her throat. The Wolf stood between them but didn't move or growl. She knew she would see him again. He had a part in this, but what? She knew they were coming back for her but didn't know how she knew. They had said nothing but she sensed fear in them but thought maybe it was the animals or the spirit they feared. She would miss them.

The Governor

He had sent his wife and daughter to take a vacation on a train ride. The train had just been completed into the west with a new station, hotel and small city at the end. It was safe, they told him. The Indians had retreated. Stories of them praying for a prophecy to be fulfilled had them all in quiet prayer. What had happened? The train had stopped for water. Louise had gotten off the train to pick some berries for her mother when the attack happened. His wife was safe. The small group of train guards helped hold off the attack. The Indians were not as determined as before. They seemed to get what they wanted and left. Now they new it was <u>Louise</u>.

He loved his wife and their combined love gave birth in a daughter Louise. There wasn't a moment of the day he didn't think of her. She was the heart of his life; she was what made her mother and him remember all their love.

The doctor made her mother sleep. He had tried to calm her but couldn't. He had heard the stories of the legend. Was it to be Louise? Was she to be the Indian miracle? She was his miracle and he wanted her back, even with a child. Anything from her would be a wonder.

As a father he feared for her. She was still a young girl; she just started learning about being a woman. Please God, don't let them hurt her. Please keep her safe.

When she was a child, she would sit on his knee and she would tell him she wasn't afraid because he was here to protect her. Please God help her not to be afraid.

He had sent the old army scout and his son to find her. He hoped they could and that they would be bringing her home. But the other part of him knew something big was going down and she was part of it. He prayed she would still be alive when it was over.

He heard men coming; it was the old scout and his son. He hoped it would be good news but he felt his stomach turn and his heart beat fast. Part of him was afraid to hear and part of him couldn't wait. Please God if she is dead help us to accept it.

The old man was telling him she was alive. He also told him of how the animals were her protection. He told him of the white Wolf and Bear. He knew in his heart that something was happen that he did not understand. He felt he was to be part of this, but he didn't want to be. He wanted his daughter back.

The scout told him his daughter seemed happy and ready for what ever was to come; she didn't remember her past but she welcomed her future. He said he felt like she had more knowledge and understanding of nature and the Indians than she could have learned in the short time. He felt she was possessed by a spirit. He felt stupid in saying it but he did believe it. He told him she wasn't afraid. Thank God for that. She knew she was to have a child for the Indians but didn't know what would happen after that.

He just took it all in. The whole thing seemed like a dream. Two weeks ago, Louise and her mother were planning what to wear on their trip. He remembered the laughs and smiles as they planned being together on a train trip. Only a train trip, not a new life.

The scout felt they must save her, but didn't honesty know how. If they could get past the Indians, then there were all the animals to deal with. She loved the animals so they couldn't kill them; and, even if they got past all that, what about the spirit. He wouldn't let her go. She would fight all the way but still they needed to go get her and bring her home. The scout had told him he had promised his son he would go back and bring her home. He had to, or the boy wouldn't leave. The governor realized the boy loved his daughter already. It was easy for him to understand; after all, she was his daughter.

The scout recommended they send for more help. She was safe for now and they didn't have enough power to overtake all the Indians. If he sent for help, they could plan an attack and learn more about the legend so they knew what they were dealing with. It made sense even though he didn't want to wait. He knew it was for the best. It would do no good for them all to die.

He called for a soldier to deliver his letter to the fort. The fort was four days ride (if it got through). He would ask for them to send all they could and they would. Not only because he was governor and this was his child, but because they wanted to rid themselves of the Indians and this was a good excuse. The army had wanted to kill all the Indians for years. He had stopped them. He was the one who said they should be all as one; that this had been their home before the White man. He felt peace would come and knowledge of White and Red would make a better world. Now he was asking them to come and kill the red man to get his daughter back.

He couldn't help it. He needed his child and so did her mother. Maybe God would forgive him. He knew he would never forgive himself. Maybe just by seeing a large army they would go. But somehow, he knew this wouldn't happen.

Once he got her back, he would spend the rest of his term as governor trying to make the Red and White get along.

The scout said they needed time to learn about the legend but he already knew. He remembered hearing about it when he had gone from camp to camp trying to bring hope to the Indians and White for a future together. He remembered thinking how all oppressed people wanted a great leader. They were waiting for the greatest leader of all. He was to save them. He would have all the knowledge of the past. The Great Spirit would be part of him. But the governor felt that spirit was with his daughter now. If she was the mother of their future, he was the grandfather. He would take her and the boy and keep them safe. Maybe this wasn't the spirit's plan, but it was his and he was her father and if he could help it, she wouldn't be the mother of the Indian's future, just the mother, someday of his grand children.

He knew he had to deal with this spirit. But he had his God. He would pray that he could bring his daughter back in body and mind. If this spirit was good maybe he could reason with it, perhaps not. Either way she was coming home.

He knew why he had picked Louise: from the day she was born she loved everything and everybody only finding good in people. Her smile always ready and her heart always open. If God had planned this, he wished he would have known. Not that it would make it easier but at least he would know it was a good spirit with her. He feared she would be led on the wrong path because she saw no bad in anything or anyone. Maybe it too, would love her and not want to give her up. He could understand how this might happen but prayed that it would not.

How do you fight a spirit? He needed to pray for help. He knew that this was something he had no control over. When he heard his wife dreaming of her grandchild. Her little red skinned grandchild. God help them.

The courier left with the letter. He went to talk to the young man. The scouts son an army man. His dad, the old scout, had taken him along to find Louise but the boy was a Captain. The boy was smitten with Louise. He wanted to just go and get her. He couldn't see that there was no hope that way. He seemed almost possessed.

He was a man on his way up. He not only knew all the right

people but was also an excellent and talented officer. He had gone to all the right schools, lived through all the right battles and now was faced with a great test. The governor must help him through this. He could see the boy was frightened for Louise and wanted to bring her home. When he had met his wife, he loved her at once too. Maybe this young man was part of all this too. Maybe he could help after. Maybe he would love her even with another man's child. That would be too much to ask, but looking into the boys' eyes he could see that maybe he wouldn't have to ask.

He didn't have to ask. The boy said he wanted to bring her back and make her is wife. He knew that he must sound a bit loco but he loved her from the moment he saw her. He knew he could make her love him. He knew what the Indian said would happen and he didn't care. He wanted her anyway even with an Indian baby. When he first set his eyes on her in front of that cabin with the Wolf, he knew there would be no other. Ever since that moment he couldn't close his eyes or sleep without being filled with thoughts and images of her. She was his destiny. With her he could be all he could be: she made his heart smile. He new this was right. Louise and he would be one.

He hoped her father would help him but knew even if he didn't understand he still must try.

The governor told him of his plans and said if he really meant what he said it would be a great solution for the problem of a future for his daughter.

When the boy left the governor sat by his wife and cried. God help them all.

The Love

The day after the trappers left, Louise woke up feeling very at peace. The Wolf was sleeping beside her. He was a beautiful animal, so strong and yet so gentle with her. She heard a sound and the Wolf lifted his head and rose. He went to the door and when she opened it, he walked out and left the cabin. As she looked outside, she saw about 10 Indian women approaching the cabin. Some young like her and some much older. They said nothing; keeping their eyes down. They made almost no noise. They brought with them rugs, blankets and clothing, all with markings of some strange sort. They looked like stories put on cloth with Indian figures. They cleaned and redid the cabin so that it looked like a drawing she had seen of the inside of a tepee. The woman also brought food and wood. They began to sing a song she didn't understand. But it was a melody that made her calm and she sat in the chair and watched them. She had no fear. She knew they were here to make ready the promise of the ancient ones. She knew she was part of this strange prophecy and seemed at peace with it.

At mid morning they took her to the stream to bathe her. They washed her hair and braided it just like theirs. Then they took her to the cabin and dressed her in an Indian robe and beaded her hair. Then they gave her some food and when she was done eating, they made her lie down on the bed. They continued to chant. She could feel the warmth of the fire and felt sleepy.

When she woke up it was dark and the Wolf and Bear were nowhere to be seen. She felt like she was alone and was a little frightened. She felt the spirit was not with her.

She had heard the drums and chants and arose from the bed and went to the door.

He was walking to the cabin. There were about 50 with him: the learned ones, the young braves, the old ones and he felt the spirit in him. They were going to the young White woman. He was to fulfill the prophecy. He was to bring them the flesh of the prophecy, but all he felt was longing. He wanted her; his body ached with want and desire and the chants and drums were ringing in his head and he wondered if he still was in a trance and a sleep.

He saw the cabin and she stood at the door. She was beyond his idea of beauty. She looked like pure white snow, wild like the wind, and soft like fur, bright like the stars, he didn't know why he was chosen but seeing her he was glad.

The Indians had made a circle around the cabin. She could see the young chief not far away. He was the most handsome man she had ever seen. He wore a feather head dress and a loin cloth. His chest was bare and his body was perfect. His chest was massive and solid. The muscles were well toned. His hair was pitch black and was just below his shoulders. She felt excitement and longing but also, she wondered where the spirit went. She could feel his absence and knew what was to come was to be without him. It frightened her. And she lowered her head in fear.

He walked up to her and took her chin in his warm strong hands and lifted her head. They were inches apart. She looked into his eyes and saw all the madness but also, she saw the spirit. He was with the young chief and he had come to her in the flesh. She almost lost her breath. She backed into the cabin and he followed. The chants and drums outside continued and seemed to fill her thoughts.

He closed the door. Here she was alone with him. He had followed her to kill her and now she was to be his wife. But not like the one he would have had as an Indian; not one to do his wishes to take care of his needs, but one to love and be his equal.

The cabin was filled with glimmering light. Making everything seemed unreal. His body looked almost shimmering; she looked into his eyes and knew she was to have her lover in another person's body. The excitement in her made her shiver. She looked at his body in front of her. His body was perfect, very broad shoulders and a small waist. His physique was almost frightening. His face looked stern with ragged lines and the sharp bone structure of an Indian. All this alone was very frightening but when she looked into his eyes, she saw all the love in him. She saw her friend and lover in this man's body.

He saw her beauty like a plunge into a cold stream. He was awakened by sheer lust mixed with so much love that he knew the spirit in him owned her love and the two of them would take her body.

He stood inches from her now and she could feel his breath and the warmth of his body. She wanted him to touch her. She felt if he didn't soon, she would faint, but he just looked at her. She felt him touch her body first only with his eyes and then, with gentleness she had never known, he placed his lips on hers.

When their lips met their flesh became one. They breathed as one. They thought as one, and couldn't get close enough. They explored each other's flesh and minds. It was as if time had stopped and their love was all the world was about.

They couldn't talk in words but they communicated with their bodies and minds. He spent hours just holding her close to him, looking at her and trying to figure out a way to keep her. The spirit in him had never felt such love. This love was strong enough to save his people. He knew this time with her must end. It must be given up but he, the young chief, would give all if it could last.

It was a new love, fresh for the-first-time love, exploring each other, wanting to please and wanting to be pleased. Not remembering before and wanting to plan what was to come, smiling, laughing, touching and all the time knowing it would end forever. That all they would have would be memories and a child.

The young chief wanted more. He wanted many children and he wanted to make a home for his woman; yes, his woman. How did you give up someone who has become part of you? He needed her and he knew she needed him. He must make a plan. He must get them out of here. He could go to the mountains. They could live up there. No one would find them; he could take care of her. He would provide for her and his child. That's the way it was supposed to be. That's what he had learned from his tribe. Now that he had taken this woman, she was his forever. She belonged to him and he owned her. He also took on the reasonability of taking care of her for life. He wanted this and, in his heart, he knew she wanted this too.

She found herself loving the chief also. He was gentle and loving. She felt safe within his arms, and knew he was her other self. He made her feel feminine, pretty and smart. She knew he felt the same. Some how maybe they could change this and stay together. Maybe they, together, could teach his people; after all, the spirit was with him. Like this she had both. She loved both and the thought of losing either made her feel lost and lonely. She knew in her heart this was her mate. She could love another but never be his mate. This young chief, and the spirit in him, was her mate for life and even though she tried to convince herself they would be together forever she knew it would soon only be a memory.

Without the spirit in her she began to remember the past. She remembered first her mother, sweet, loving and always there. She missed her. So far all she could remember was her face and how she felt about her. Maybe more would come with time. How would her mother feel about her mate? She didn't know, but it really didn't matter. One loved for one self. She would never stop loving this man and spirit and never regret these weeks together. She had found true love of mind and body and together the three of them, her young chief and the spirit, and her would make a child. With all their love, he would be great.

He would be the reason to go on and care; she wondered what her dreams as a child were. She must have thought of being in love and having children. She was sure she didn't even think she would be in love with a child to raise alone.

He was trying to make her understand something. For days he had pointed at the mountains. She thought maybe he meant they would go there. She wished it could be true but she knew in her heart that all they tried would be against the prophecy and she wondered how you could change a prophecy. When do your dreams outweigh that of a nation?

He lay beside her, sleeping. The fire light glimmered and her eyes filled with tears and she looked at the man she loved and part of her knew he was lost to her and she felt it would be soon. Softly she said, "I love you now, always, and forever and your child might not know you in flesh but will through my heart." She laid close to him and felt his arms around her all night. In the morning they made love. It was different, almost sad. After he took her outside and pointed to the mountain. He was trying to tell her he was going to the mountains to set up camp and find a safe place for them and that he would come back for her. He knew she didn't understand but would do what he wanted. Oh, how he loved her. She was the only one who had brought love to his heart. He no longer thought of Red and White, just two people in love on a journey into life. He must make them be together forever.

The spirit knew it was their last day as flesh together. He must get the young chief to go to the mountains. He must make him believe there was hope. The spirit knew that when the young chief returned Louise would be gone and that he would probably never see her again. If a spirit could cry, he would. He new the journey that they must take was without the young chief and he would still love Louise but never be able to touch her, kiss her to feel her body one with his. How could he bear this? How could he give this up? But all the power of the old ones made him realize this must be.

    Louise sat on the steps watching the young chief go toward the mountains. The spirit was with him and she had lost them both. Just as she was ready to run after him, she heard the Indian women. They were coming back again. She felt sick and drugged and the Indian women took her into the cabin and took care of her for days.

The Captain

The captain had received the message from the governor. After all the heat he had taken from him for killing Indians, now he wanted them killed. I guess his daughter was a reason. But what about all the other people's relatives killed by the Indians. They were supposed to forgive? He should tell him no, but he knew this was a great opportunity that might not come again. His wife and child were killed by the savages. He wanted them all dead and he didn't care what excuse he had to use.

He knew they would probably find her dead. He had seen what they did to white women. He hoped if she was alive that God would let her forget. He felt death would probably be better.

He would need to make a plan; maybe he would need to kill her if the damage done to her was bad enough. He would if he needed to. He didn't want any young woman to live with that kind of memory. He hoped he would find her before the Indians had time to hurt her and maybe he wouldn't have to kill her.

His army had reached the train and the governor was waiting. He listened to the governor and actually felt sad for him. He understood the worry, and he understood the fear of what was happening to her. He remembered waiting and worrying and finding your worst thoughts coming true.

He would help him even though he resented him for not helping him. The governor was telling them he wanted no killing, they must only shoot if shot at. This man was trying his patience. He was going to kill no matter what the governor thought. He would let him believe whatever he had too. The governor could sleep at night thinking he had not been part of the killing. But his daughter would give him the power to kill them all and if they had killed her, he knew the governor would look the other way. Everyone has strong morals until they have to be the moral one. He would be able to manipulate him. He could get his own way.

Their scouts told him of a great number of Indians camped around the old cabin where the girl was. Maybe she was bait. Maybe they were using her to get the army all in one place so they could massacre them. It didn't matter what their plan was for he would have a better one. He was White and he had more knowledge than that bunch of red men.

The night he found his wife and child who always went through his thoughts and dreams. He never would get the picture out of his mind. These were not men. They were beasts. Killing them was like killing bugs. They didn't deserve an after thought.

His plan was simple; get the girl dead or alive and, on the way, kill as many Indians as they could. The first step was to send the scout and his son back to protect her when the attack started. The boy would be glad to go; you could tell he loved her. Just like the captain had loved his wife. This way the boy would be able to protect her. He couldn't protect his wife and child. He would give this chance to the boy.

Usually, the army just marched in blowing horns and shouting, but not this time. This time it would be different. First, they would send the scout to find all the camps around the cabin, and then they would circle them. Slowly, at night, they could move in and kill every Indian they could find. His men were really like him, they were tired of waiting too. So, they could taste the kill.

They would wait and leave in the morning after the scouts were back and he was sure the boy and his father were with the governor's daughter.

He didn't sleep all night. All he could see was his wife holding his child with blood all over, so much blood. Oh, God could he ever forget. His whole life all gone: all his hopes, dreams and plans gone forever. He must avenge them. It was his time.

The sun rose slowly. You could see the mist almost like steam evaporating off the ground. The birds began the morning with singing. He wondered if he would ever feel like singing again but he new the answer. You couldn't sing when your song is dead; and his was.

He saw the governor pacing in his tent. It was still dark enough that the light within showed shadows. He too, must be thinking of his song, his daughter, and praying she still could sing.

He must get his plan down and send for his army. This day would hold victory over death. Inside a peace over took him, and he knew today the nightmare would end.

They all sat in the tent looking at the captain's plan. The scouts told him the Indians were camped in a circle around the back of the cabin about a mile away. The thing the scouts found funny was all the learned ones, chiefs and braves, were directly across the cabin on the other side of the river. They had left their women and children unprotected. The army would cross the river five miles south of the circle behind the braves. At the same time, he would have the other half come from behind the cabin. Since no braves were there to stop them, they would have them in a cross fire.

The governor felt that they could just get Louise and leave; but he felt they could start a battle to end the red man from ever hurting another White woman.

The Cave

He had gone up into the mountains. He must hurry. He knew her people could come for her anytime and his people, believing in the prophecy, would let them take her.

The very thought of life without her was like a knife plunged into his heart. To believe he could love like this was almost like a dream. As a young man he was raised to be a chief. They did not show emotion or pity or even love. But he knew the spirit in him was also lost in her love.

He did know he had to find the cave. He had hidden in it as a child. He would have strange dreams of a White woman and a child. He would see the child being dressed up like a White man. It would make him feel he was crazy and he would run to the mountains and find the cave and pray to the spirits to help him.

The cave was about the size of a small tepee. He had made a fire pit in the middle years ago. He would come up here to just think. He noticed his paintings on the walls. They showed his journey, showing his youth, his becoming a chief and a child and then nothing. Oh, he was young. He couldn't have known about Louise. He wasn't going to lose her. Here in the mountains, there was water and food and there would be great love. That he would paint on the walls of the cave. She loved him, not the spirit. He knew it. He felt her body and mind become one with his flesh. She loved him and needed his love to survive. They would be happy here. His people would see his wise decision and follow him, and the boy would grow up and dress as an Indian not a White. He would be taught like his father and he would save his people. He would be a great chief.

First, he must get the cave ready. He didn't want Louise to be cold or hungry. He remembered at night when she slept. He could just look at her and be happy and if that peace in him could last forever, what more could he want. But as a warrior he knew you had to fight for your life and protect your family.

He knew she was with child already. The spirit in him told him the second the child came into being. It is his son, not the spirits. The future was from his and her flesh, just the two of them.

He could make her happy. She seemed like an angel without a worry or want; she accepted all that was around her. She must have had a very different life before this. She must have family. Would she remember and want to leave? He and his people would be her family. They would make her forget and the child would make her part of him.

How did he explain her beauty? Yes; soft skin, round breast, gentle curves, silky hair, wonderful pure smile; but, look in her eyes and there was the beauty. Deep in her eyes you could see her pure soul, the wonderment of life and the oneness of nature. No, he would not lose her and no one would take her from him.

He tried to tell her he was gong into the mountains to make a home. She seemed to understand. He hoped she knew he was coming back for her. She must because she smiled and gently kissed his check as he left. He could still feel her lips on his face.

All of a sudden, he felt something was wrong. The spirit had left him. He could feel it. What did this mean? No, not that? He started to run down the mountain. He could hear his every breath and foot step but, in his heart, he knew it was too late.

Alone

She sat alone on the front step of the cabin. He was going to the mountains. She was sure he was going to make a place for him and her, but did he know she had his seed? She put her head in her hands and cried. They were gone both of them. She knew deep inside she would never see the young chief again. She wanted to run after him but she knew that would only bring sadness down life's road. Would the spirit, her best friend, come back? Did he love or use her or just need her? Part of her didn't care. She loved him even though she knew he was many spirits in one. He had made her see the goodness in everything, even herself. When he was with the young chief, he could make all her dreams of love come true, the dreams of a young girl of perfect love. Sweet and tender, knowing you are loved and loving back. But she also knew it was only for a short time and this time she had with them must last forever in her heart. And she would keep it in her heart and that was better than never feeling the great joy it had brought to her.

The Indian women still came and took care of her, but she felt alone, no one to talk to: no one who would look into her eyes. They were afraid of the spirit and they did not know if he was with her or the young chief.

The Wolf came back and they walked together. She talked to

him about her dreams and wants. Maybe he did understand. At night he slept close and the warmth of his body made her feel safe. She knew she would lose him also, soon very soon. How could you tell the world about all these wonderful and frightening experiences? People would think she had lost her mind. She had heard about what happened to White women when taken by the Indians. How could she believe she was better than they? Why her? They would all think the worst because of the baby, maybe hate the child. She could feel the sadness in her heart. How could she tell them of the great love and joy? Maybe she was crazy.

Then one morning she knew all was to change. The Indian women had left her dress, the one from the train. The one she had worn to the cabin. It was all torn and dirty. It would make people think the worst. She could hear the drums and knew her worse fears were to come true. She was going back to what used to be her home and leaving the ones she loved. The only thing that still brought her joy was the great gift she was taking with her. A boy, who had two fathers, one, a Great Spirit, of not just one tribe of Indians but all the dreams and hopes of his kind, and one, a young chief, an Apache, strong of body and mind. This would make up her son's fathers. How could she teach him the ways of the Indian? She hardly knew her way in life and now they were gone and she was very frightened

She heard horses coming. The trapper and his son had returned. The Indians had let them through. Were they to take her back? The Wolf left her side and went into the forest and she knew he was also gone to her. What sadness. Why could they not just leave her here? She would not go. The chief would be back and he would stop them.

She looked into the young trapper's son's eyes. He looked concerned. He had soft eyes. You could see the good in him. They showed no hate or anger, just concern. She could tell he wanted to ask her about what happened but was afraid to. Maybe he thought it would be too much to hear and still remain calm. What if she told him of the great love and the closeness and the child? She knew he would think she made it up to keep her self sane. The thought of no one believing her was almost too much to bear. Maybe it was all a dream and things didn't happen the way she remembered. If not, where was the spirit? Where was her lover? And then she felt him return. The spirit was with her again. Her heart almost burst and her body shivered. The young man put a blanket around her and held her close. She cried. He thought from fear but it was from great joy. She would be alright with him with her. She could face anything; her lover had returned.

The Plan

The plan was to keep the Indians out of the cabin while the captain surrounded them. The captain knew that the Indians thought a prophecy was being fulfilled and, most likely, they would try to take her. Part of him wondered why they had let him and his dad in; why they hadn't moved her where she couldn't be found. There were many places that the red man knew that they did not.

He could read the drums; the young chief had planted his seed in the women. Where had he gone? Did he just come and rape her and leave? No, the drums talked of days. Maybe she didn't remember. But she was crying so maybe she did.

He had followed in his father's footsteps and joined the army very young. He was a good trapper; not as great as his dad yet, but close. He had worked his way up in the army, retired as a lieutenant and had gone to school and now was a lawyer. He had heard of the train attack and had come to help his father find this girl. He had never met her but knew of her father. He was a good, kind man who worked for peace, just like him.

He had spent most of his young life working and learning about life but not living it. He had not loved or even noticed a woman; but now he loved one he had only seen twice. He didn't know much about her. Maybe she was a spoiled girl wanting every thing done for her and playing the smile game. No, he knew that wasn't true. She was kind and loving and now she had been hurt and must feel frightened. He couldn't change what had happened to her but maybe he could help her get through it. What they did to her was not who she was. She was an innocent. Some people would look down at her because of the baby to come. He would love her and the baby because the baby was part of her. First, he must become her friend and hope he could help her by being her husband. First, he would be a friend and then maybe she could learn to love him. Either way he knew this was his path in his life. Her father would help him. Her being with child would ruin her life without a husband. The child would be an outcast. What a tragedy this story seemed to be. What kind of a prophecy was this? All this hate must stop. It just ruined lives. Why couldn't people just get along even though they were different, but: first things first. He must get her, and them, out of there alive.

As she cried in his arms, he gently rocked her. He told her his name was Bill. He told her all would be alright. That she should just try to forget what had happened and think of going home with people who loved her. He would help her and stay by her side. He wouldn't let anyone hurt her anymore.

She wanted to say, "I love him. He didn't hurt me. I want him back," but the spirit stopped her. He made her understand this man was the one who would help her raise the boy. He knew all about the man. The man's heart was true and wanted peace. He would teach the child to love all kinds of people even when they were hard to love. He had the White man's knowledge and could teach the boy to learn all the books and items he would need to help make the peace, and, then, his real father would help in the end. She looked into his eyes and saw the kindness and concern for her. She could tell he hurt for her and wanted to make everything all right. The spirit was right. He was a good man. She would do what the spirit wanted because she loved the spirit and believed in all the things, he taught her. She looked at him and told him all would be alright.

He looked into her eyes and worried who was looking back at first; and, then they changed and he saw her there again. What had they done to her to make her believe so much in the future? Maybe her tears were not that of an abused woman but one who felt a loss. Even if they had made her think differently, she had been abused, and this was not her will. She had been used and even if it was for the good of many it was wrong without her consent. He believed in peace but how could taking someone from their life make it alright? If she would let him, he would teach this child the way to begin a life of peace between both his families. But he must remember he had to get them out alive. He knew he must watch the captain. He had been hurt beyond reason so he was not to be trusted. He could feel it was better to kill her then have her live with what he knew his wife had gone through. No, he must watch him. The plan would start in the morning and he would not leave Louise's side. The drums were still telling a story, one of victory. Were they going to fight for her or was she, their victory? His father had made a great fire and some soup. He got her to eat and lie down and she went into a deep sleep while the drums became louder and louder.

The Attack

The captain didn't sleep all night; he could feel the sweat of hate on his body. He couldn't get the picture of his wife and child out of his mind. She didn't want to come out west with him she wanted to stay in the city. She told him she was afraid. He had laughed at her and told her not to be a child, that, he would be there to protect her. That conversation would never leave his mind, never. He wasn't there to protect her and couldn't forgive himself.

Where he was stationed was far from where the fighting was going on. They were at a fort not too far west. She and the boy had gone for a walk by the river. They had done this often, seemed perfectly safe. Who knew? A band of renegade Indians were out to show the White man not to enter their land. They took his wife and killed the boy. He searched for three days and then found her. She hadn't been dead long. They kept her alive. Did she hate him those three days for not being there? He hated himself. He hated and hated. It ate at his insides.

He wanted to find her alive, but after seeing her body and what was done to her, he was glad she was dead and didn't have to remember. His punishment was to remember.

Tomorrow he would get his revenge, they would all die. The sun was coming up and just shadows could be seen. His scout told him the old man and the boy were in the cabin. The drums had been loud all night, but now there was only silence. Were they ready for them? He had wondered why they had let the old man and boy get close to her. Something was not right about all this.

He, too, had heard the story. That one was to come, to bring peace to White and Red man. Peace? He had no peace and knew he never would. But what if this was true? No more killing, no more hatred, no more pain. Who was he kidding? The hate was too deep to fix. How could he forgive? Why would he forgive? People told him the anger and hate that filled him was why he suffered and that if he could rid himself of the guilt and anger, he would be able to continue his life with some peace. Did they lose a wife, a child? What right did they have telling him to forgive and how did they think he could forget?

He looked out his tent and saw the governor passing around the camp. He knew how he must feel, but still he had a strong dislike for him, always saying we needed to get along with the Indians. I wonder how he feels now?

He left his tent and told his scouts to go and check around the cabin. He wanted to make sure nothing had changed. He had good soldiers; they would do as he said. If he said kill all, they would. But he didn't want them to have to kill the women and children so he had given the order to take all the women and children to a camp where their men could worry and wonder what was happening to them. This made him smile.

He would have to get into the cabin before her father got there. If she needed his help to die, her father might try to stop him. He would make it quick. Much better than a life with memories that haunted your mind and soul. He would help her because he couldn't help his wife and child.

The scouts were returning and he went to meet them. Very strange, they were telling him all the Indians were gone and the cabin looked like nothing had happened to it. They could see the smoke and light from the fire pit in the cabin. Everything looked undisturbed. They did not enter the cabin or go close for fear of an ambush. There was no sound from the cabin so they feared all were dead.

He had a hard time convincing the governor that he should wait until they could make sure it was safe. He understood that he wanted to go to his daughter. Even though he didn't like the man, he didn't want him to see what he was sure was in the cabin.

When he reached the cabin, all was silent. It almost seemed peaceful, like a picture. Or was it the silence before the awful truth. He must remember why he was there. He must find out if this young girl needed his help.

The old man opened the cabin door. They were alive. He told the captain he knew that the Indians had left in the night. He knew because the drums stopped. The drums told of the spirit's way to peace and that they should all leave. He told him the girl was sleeping and seemed in shock. His son was close beside all night, keeping watch. He told him that they could send for her father and that should make her feel better. Feel better. He would be the judge of that. He needed to talk to her first. He entered the cabin and saw her lying on the bed. Bill, the young man, was just looking at her. He could tell how much he cared just by his face. He had to get him out of the cabin so if he needed to kill her, no one would stop him. He told Bill and his father to go and get her father and he would stay with her until they returned. Bill didn't want to go. He was afraid of the captain and what he might do. Everyone knew what he had been through and the hatred in his heart. He would send his father and stay outside the cabin and watch.

Louise woke up and was startled to see the captain. Where were Bill and his dad? The Spirit in her told her to be careful, there was danger. She sat up and looked into his eyes and saw all the hurt.

She wanted to hold him and tell him all would be ok but also saw the hate and knew nothing she would say would change his heart. He looked at the dress on the chair. It was all torn and he thought the worst. She spoke to him and told him she was ok. They had not hurt her, but she could see he didn't believe her. You might think know you're not hurt but wait until you remember. The dreams will haunt you and if there is a child you will have to bear all the shame. He pulled his knife out of its sheaf and very slowly moved behind her. He would make it quick and she would not have the shame and dreams. He did not see Bill come from behind him and take him to the ground. As he fell, he saw his wife and child call to him. His chest hurt and he closed his eyes and went to them. His heart had stopped and so had all his hurt.

Bill took Louise in his arms and held her close and the door opened and her father came in and ran to her with tears and smiles. He was told the captain had a heart attack and was at peace at last.

When he looked into his daughter's eyes, he realized something was different. She did not seem frightened. She looked in good health and she smiled at him with extreme warmth. He wanted to get her out of there as fast as he could but he also wanted not to upset her anymore than needed. He must make sure the Indians stayed gone before they returned to the train and her mother. Her mother was where Louise had gotten her beauty. He loved her from the first time he saw her and, when they had Louise, he was the happiest man on Earth. Life was perfect. But the last few weeks in his life had changed the way he looked at things. Things you love can be taken away without a moment's notice and lost forever. He thought of all the time he had spent becoming governor. All the time away from the two people he loved most. He felt he had been given a second chance. It was time to take his child home and hope and pray she could forget or at least cope with what had happened. He had brought clean clothes for her. He didn't want her mother ever to see the dress she had worn. He hoped it was from the trip through the forest to get to the cabin that had torn and soiled it, but part of him didn't want to know. She changed her clothes and unbraided her hair. He could see why Bill loved her. She was so beautiful, and not just her looks. You could almost see her heart. Something had happened here and maybe someday she could tell him.

They started to leave the cabin and the drums started again. He hesitated but Bill told him they were telling the spirit to have a safe journey and to take care of the women and child because their future was in his hands.

Going Home

They had not thought to bring a wagon for Louise. She was a city girl and riding horses was not something she had ever done. Bill thought he would just have her ride on the back of his horse but as they got near the horses, the captain's horse, a beautiful black stallion, came up to her and rested its face against hers. She put her foot in the stirrup and mounted the horse, as if she had ridden one all her life. Well, he better get used to this spirit person being part of their lives because it looked like he, or it, was here to stay. Let's hope he or it wasn't jealous. The horse began to trot with its head held high like it knew something we didn't and that it carried someone we didn't know; someone very important. Maybe the horse thought this spirit was special but Bill was thinking of Louise. She was very special to him. No matter who was walking with her, she was picked out because of how special she was and would always be. He could see her father with great wonder as he watched her ride off on the great stallion. It would be very hard to see your daughter and wonder who she had become. You could still see the innocence in her but also felt the presence of something or someone with great knowledge.

When they arrived at the train her mother ran to her, at first startled by the great horse, but then like a mother just glad to hold her again without question.

As Louise sat on the train taking her home, she thought, Home? Where was that? She was making a home with the one she loved. He had entered the young chief and they were one. She knew now the spirit was with her again. He had left the young chief and was part of her again. She loved him (or was this love of many) the legend said many. Her mind was like a whirly wind. How did she make sense out of all this? She saw her father look at her with so much sadness. She knew he thought she was raped, but how could she tell him: she was loved? How could she tell him of her great love, and that it was bringing her a son? A baby who was part his father the chief, and part the spirit. They would think her mad and maybe she was. Her mother just held her in her arms and the tears that fell from her eyes touched Louise's face. In her heart she wanted to say please don't cry I am happy.

When her father looked at her, he saw his daughter of eighteen who had lost her innocent. She was not alone in her mind. Was there a spirit or had she just gone mad? All she had been through would make anyone mad. If the story were true, she was with child. He had always dreamed of a grand child but not in this way. What would he be like? Would he be a spirit or a child? Would he love them or use them? What ever happened he would love him because he was part of his daughter and that was good enough for him. As he watched her, she fell asleep in her mother's arms. She really did look like an angel asleep. Maybe all would be ok. The train kept traveling to the east and he wished he had never taken his wife and daughter west. But that was the past. He now needed to look at the future. He must talk to Bill. Maybe he would help. Bill loved her, you could tell that in his face, and he didn't think the child would matter to him, but would she let them fulfill their plan? Bill would marry her and say they fell in love at first sight. The wedding would be next week. No one would think a thing about the baby not being Bill's. Not even his wife. At least she would be happy with the grandchild and never think of how it came to be. He didn't think his wife could live through remembering every time she looked at the baby what had happened to her daughter. This would be better. Please Lord let her say yes.

The Wedding

The wedding was grand. All the guests felt the governor had gotten his daughter back unharmed. The story of the brave captain who gave his life for her was on every- body's mind. People told how the young Bill and Louise had fallen in love at first sight when he had come with the captain to rescue her.

Louise and Bill looked the perfect couple: he a young handsome man, with a wonderful future; and she just beautiful. Bill knew the love he had for her she didn't share. But he also knew she liked and cared for him. When her father had told her of their plan to have her marry Bill so she wouldn't have to face the sorrow of people knowing what had happened to her, she had agreed because the spirit had told her to. She felt everyone should know what had happened to her. The wonderful experience with all the animals and the great care of the Indians and of course the great love she had shared with the chief. But the spirit had told her no. That people would view the child as a sorrow and that would hinder his path. So, she had agreed. She liked Bill and, because it was what the spirit wanted, she would make him a good wife. He had told her he would be her husband and take care of her and the child but knew that the rest of the marriage would take time and he would wait because being with her was better then not seeing her.

Bill knew of the prophecy and wanted to help her with the child because if it was part of her, he already loved the boy. How had she known he was a boy? He didn't know but he did believe her. He felt at times there was a part of her he did not know. If it was a spirit, it was allowing him to love her and take her for his wife and he was thankful for that. If there was a spirit, maybe it would be with the baby and when the child was born Louise would be free to love him. But, either way, he would take whatever he could get and be happy just to be close to her.

The wedding was the talk of the town. Her father had spared no expense. He was just glad she was back and Bill was helping him protect her. If people learned the story, they would think her mad. She did her part. She stood close to Bill held his arm and even looked at him with great affection, but when he looked at her, he could see that some thing or some one was calling the shots. Most of the people there were living in their own little world and not aware of what was going on outside of their lives. The women: housewives, daughters and children were kept from hearing disturbing things: the men didn't believe half of what they heard and could easily blame everything on others. Had he been like that? He had fought for justice but was it all lip service? What if they had killed her? What of justice then? Thank you, Lord, for not giving me that decision to make. He had sent a mad man to save her. The captain was going to kill her. Why? The reason died with him but he hoped it was to save her from the memories, not to get even with her father. He and the captain went way back. The captain's idea of dealing with the Indian problem, as he called it, was to just kill them and then there would be no problem. They had gone round and round about how to end this war and he was sure the captain hated him and the hate grew deeper after his wife and child were killed. The scouts told them that the Indians that did this were young bucks that had formed their own group and their idea of life was to get all they could no matter who it hurt. He had been looking for the persons who were giving them alcohol, and as of yet had not found them. The scouts told him the main group of Indians were also looking for them, not to arrest them but to bring their own justice.

His life from now on would be different than he would have ever expected. What if the child looked Indian? What if the chief came after her? He needed to quit with all the worry and try to enjoy the fact he had her back.

Her mother was talking to Louise and smiling. They looked a lot alike. Not very long ago his wife was close to madness with worry and know so very happy. She kissed their daughter on the cheek and a tear dropped down her face and for a moment he could see she remembered how close they had come to losing her. Being a mother, he was sure she knew about the baby. Louise and her mother are close. She would have told her all about what happened. Her mother would listen and hope it was true and not just a way to forget the bad, but deep inside, hope her daughter wasn't going mad. When Louise was a young girl, her mother worried about the man she would marry and, now, we had to worry about a spirit and a man I knew loved her and that I hoped would not come for her and the baby.

The spirit took all this in. It was very hard for him to see Bill next to Louise but he knew that this was for the best. Part of him never wanted her to love anyone else and part of him loved her so much he wanted her happy and maybe when he joined with the child she could go on with her life. She was so young to have all this happen to her. It was never told he would love the woman. He was just to use her for the child. And then there was the chief. He loved her also. Would he listen to what the spirit told him about not coming after her, or would he let the madness of love overtake him. The child had to be raised by these people. After being with Louise he realized they only looked and talked different. They wanted the same things his people wanted. They wanted peace and safety for the families. Oh yes, some were bad and some of his people were bad also but most were just trying to get through life and keep their families and friends safe and happy.

    There would be much sorrow, until the boy became of age and, for his father, great nights of depression and longing. You might know you are doing the best for everyone else but there are long nights when you want your dreams to come true also. He knew even as a spirit he wanted to change the way things were and be with Louise. He could enter Bill but that would only make him never enter the child. No, he too must give up what he wanted for the better of all.

Lost

When the young chief got back to the cabin Louise was gone. He entered and saw where the captain had fallen. The drums told the tale; he was going to kill her. Would he have done the same with an Indian woman if he thought she had been abused? No, to kill one's own was wrong. The drums told of the raid on the captain's family. The Indians in that group were not from any tribe. They were being hunted by all the tribes. These Indians were making the Whites think the red man were savages who had no rules of life. This wasn't true: maybe their Gods were different in name but the red man was more a part of nature and life than any White man. The thought that they could have found Louise made him understand the captain's thoughts. He would have hunted them down and killed them also. And he would have killed them very slowly. He would find these savages and end their terror. To lose one you love is bad, but like that he could see how one's mind would lose all ability to make a reasonable decision. You would just go mad and want them dead.

The drums told how the captain tried to kill her from coming behind with a knife and the young man had saved her. When he thought of this he could hardly breathe. He knew what the raiders had done to the captain's wife and child. He must have thought the same had happened to her and wanted to end the memories. He would never lose the memories. He could still smell her and if he closed his eyes, he could see her lying beside him looking into his eyes with great love. How could he ever go on with life without her? When the spirit had left him, he told him not to follow her. How did someone let they're very being just go away? She carried his child, his son, the son of a chief. The future turned over to White men. That was madness.

Outside the cabin the learned ones had gathered and built a fire. He knew they wouldn't stop him if he went after her but he also knew the prophecy would not be fulfilled. He must do what was best for his people even if it meant his life would be empty. He went outside and joined his people thanking the Gods for allowing the spirit to live among them and bring peace. He didn't know how this would be done but he believed. They gathered around him and crowned him with the head-dress of a chief. He could almost see Louise in the fire, dancing and smiling at him. He too felt like he was going mad: but he knew in the morning he would start his part in the plan for peace, and the first thing to do was to find the renegade Indians and stop them.

His father was a great chief. He had told him of the prophecy and how the spirit of the Indian nations would come to help save his people from the iron horse and the White men. He was sure his father thought a warrior was coming to battle them not a White woman and a small child. He used to wish he was to be part of the tale and now he was and wished he wasn't. Being part of something great made a person have to give up their own wants for others and he wanted Louise but that almost seemed already a dream. Some place he had entered into in a dream and found great peace and love and then wandered out again.

He would make a great warrior because he had learned all the ways of a chief and had gone through all the trials but letting go of Louise was the one trial he could almost not do. When he was a young boy, he thought the trials were to make him brave and not afraid to fight or get physically hurt. He had no idea what pain it could be to have your heart hurt. This trial would take the rest of his life to get over, if then. The dawn was coming and he had to put his hurts away and go on with his work for his people.

The New Beginning

Bill was a very successful lawyer and he bought a large house near Louise's father and mother. He knew she would need them close and he felt better with her father to talk to. No one knew the challenges they had to face, but he and his father-in-law. They had all the parties and social events needed and Louise was the perfect hostess. She still had the look in her eyes of the unknown but she seemed grateful for Bill's care and love.

She began to look pregnant about five months. He could hear her talk to the child and knew the child listened and understood. If he didn't know there was a spirit with her, he would have thought she was mad; and still, at times he wondered if all he remembered was just a bad dream and she was living in that dream world.

At night he held her close and she allowed his kiss but their marriage was just a deal. He loved holding her and her skin smelled so sweet, her hair like black silk, her lips just a pinch of red enough to be something you looked at and at once wanted to kiss. Just holding her was enough for now. After the baby was born maybe she would let him physically love her.

Louise and her mother made the baby room ready. Different views on how it should look: Grandma wanted teddy bears, and mother wanted plants, trees, birds and books, lots of books. But between the two of them the room was full of teddy bears and rocking horses.

Bill remembered one day they took a walk by the river, she held his hand and talked of the way he was to help raise the boy. He must learn the way to peace through knowledge and Bill could give him that, he knew at that time he was walking with the spirit. Even though he was a strong man this was very different and once again it made him wonder if he was still dreaming. He would teach the boy and he would love him because he was part of his mother. He needed to teach him all the ways and laws of the White. The spirit would teach him the ways of the Indian. If the spirit was in the boy, he might have a hard time keeping up with him. The spirit was many and he was just a man in love with a woman.

He had thought his life would have been like everyone else's. He had been a single man with a lot of women who thought him a great catch. He knew that, but he didn't even look at one until he saw Louise. When he saw her in the cabin, he knew that she was his mate. He never thought you would look at someone and know that but, he never again would laugh when someone told him they loved at first sight. He had seen her once before a long time ago. She was running with her father in the woods and stopping to pick flowers. He was very young but noticed her even then. He had no idea what their future was to be. This was a very hard future but he wouldn't give her up for anything. Looking back, he remembered trying to figure out what woman would be best for his future: from the right family, have the right breeding and the class he needed to get ahead in his field. And now he didn't care if they just went back and lived in the old cabin. Funny how your wants can change with just a look, a smile, just a smile but one he would carry in his heart for ever and ever. Please Lord let her love him please. He would take care of his part with the child and be what she needed him to be. But maybe someday in the future they could be one and share their old age together but for now he would be glad just to be able to hold her in his arms and see her every day and night.

    Louise had friends but none very close. They came around because her father was the governor and her husband was a very successful lawyer. They invited her to all the lady teas and afternoon parties and they were both invited to all the night celebrations. But no one was close to her. They didn't know what happened to her but all were sure it had hurt her mind. She seemed like a child in her heart. She seemed to be more interested in talking about the world around her than the pretty dresses and homes and whose husband was getting up in society. The stories heard were different then the governor had told. They didn't ask her but felt something had happened to change her way of thinking and most thought it must have been bad and that she wanted to forget it. Most felt that having this baby would probably help a lot. She could get on with being a wife and mother; after all, she had a great husband and wonderful life. Most women would die for what she had. But with all of this she still was peaceful to be around and they liked her even if they didn't understand her. They remember being jealous about her getting to go out west on a train with her mother. They remembered all the preparation with new dresses and hats. They had parties just to send her off. What had they sent her to they were not sure and probably never would be, but the young girl they knew and was their friend didn't come back, a young woman did? And even though they were not sure who she was now they still called her friend.

The Birth

The baby was born and to the wonderment of his step-father and grandpa he didn't look at all like an Indian; he had his mother's black hair and beautiful eyes. Louise didn't make a sound while going through the whole birth. Bill could see the pain in her eyes and held her hand. For being her first, it didn't take long. The boy was very healthy and had good lungs. Bill looked at his wife holding the baby and felt overcome with peace and love. Even though this wasn't his seed, this was his family and he was proud. He couldn't help but think maybe the spirit would go into the boy soon and he could try to start a new life with Louise.

When he held the child, he could feel the peace of the spirit. Maybe this child had a future already planned for him but on the way, he was going to enjoy his son.

What they couldn't hear were the drums telling of the birth. The chief called all the tribes together to celebrate the birth of his son, because he couldn't go get them, his woman and child. They had been taken away from him and were so far away he could not get to them. When he thought of all that had happened, he could hardly remain still; his insides felt like they were sick and his hands shook and his heart felt like someone had pulled it apart. Part of him wanted to scream and part of him understood what had happened. He had been given the chance only for a moment to love and be loved the way people only talked about. He would have laughed if you had told him he would feel this kind of love. He used to think it weak to love and now he understood it took great courage to give yourself to another and even more to let them go. He didn't want to let her go and at night he dreamed of holding her close and feeling his child in her. He would wake up in a sweat and search the bed for her and when he realized it was a dream he just wanted to die. He did not know how a spirit could be so cruel to him. Why did he need to love her? Why could he have just not taken her and forgot her? Why did he need to feel the sorrow? Part of him would never want to give up the memories but because of the memories part of him was dead. He would love no other and she would be his mate for life.

She would have it harder; he knew. She would have to live what her father wanted. Women did what they were told and the thought of her going to another man was almost too much to bear. He would not think of this, only of the great love she had for him. He should have taken her to the mountains with him and she would still be here with his son.

He had to forget all this. He was the leader of his tribe and must keep them safe. He could no longer kill Whites. After being with Louise he realized the White and Red were the same inside. All wanted the same things, just to live and be happy with there own beliefs. The problem was that some Whites wanted the Indian to change their beliefs and follow their beliefs and this was causing the trouble. The Whites were pushing them farther and farther west. Soon they would not even have winter camps in the mountain to go to.

There were still the Indians that left the tribes and went hunting Whites and this didn't help. He must admit at times when he thought of how they took Louise he could have killed all of them, but then he remembered that the spirit had let this happen and he

LOUISE

just was a man and didn't understand. Part of him knew he would see his son someday and he hoped Louise also. That was what kept his heart from tearing apart. Would she still love him? Would she remember, or had the spirit taken him from her heart?

It had seemed like the army had not been after them since the governor had gotten Louise back. The problem was the trappers and rebel Whites, just like their rebel Indians. They were after scalps to sell. He must get his people high up in the mountains until the prophecy was fulfilled. The boy would have to grow up and then what?

The snow was starting to fall. The snow flakes were so delicate it reminded him of her. The white snow, made him think of her skin, so pure resting on his face and her soft lips on his. The answering to his movements, the longing to be closer and the most excellent smile. The smile that made his heart beat fast and his mind have a fever of lust and love. Oh, how he missed her. Sometimes he wondered if she was a dream and never had been in his life. The boy was proof that she was in his life and they had loved and he hoped she still loved him as he loved her. He knew the spirit was with her and he knew the spirit loved her also. He envied the time the spirit spent with Louise even if it was just in her mind. Close is close. But tonight, he would celebrate the birth of his and Louise's son his people's future and tomorrow he would be the leader his people needed now. He would try to keep them from war and safe until the prophecy could be fulfilled.

He felt a smile on his lips and a thought of how can I do that? Well, he would have never thought all that had happened could be true but it was so he must be able to do his part or the spirit would have stayed with him. The drums were speaking of great joy. The beginning of the prophecy had been born and the legend was coming true. He joined his people in the celebration and kept her in his heart.

Bill

He lay in his bed. Louise was holding his hand. It had been 21 years since he had married Louise. Not one day since he first met her in the cabin out west had not been filled with great joy. Also in the room were his stepson and the spirit with him. As he closed his eyes, he remembered the boy being born. They had worried he would look like his father but he didn't, he looked like his mother. She had taught the boy how to love and Bill had taught him about justice. He wasn't sure when the spirit entered the boy, maybe just a little at a time at first. Sometimes when you would look into his eyes you would see someone with him and when I would teach him anything you could see the spirit making sure the boy understood. He didn't know when the spirit told the boy about his life, but the boy seemed to accept it. They had named him Hunter. He was to hunt for peace between his people, both White and Red.

Bill had gone back to the cabin. He wanted to see if he could find Hunter's father. The army had pushed the Indians to their limit and it seems they all were very close to war. He wanted to talk to the chief and see if they could start talking about peace. After all he had raised his son but he also had his woman and that could get him killed. He wondered how he would have felt if the chief would have gotten Louise back? He new he would hate him and want him dead. But that was before Louise told him of their great love. It was hard to hear but just the fact she was telling him made him know she cared and trusted him. She never talked about the time in the cabin before to anyone. At least the spirit had made Louise and the chief's encounter peaceful. She told a story of peace full of love and friendship. She told him of the spirit with the chief and how she loved them. She told of her great loss when she was taken back but also of the great joy with the child and how she had grown to love Bill. She loved him and that was more then he had ever hoped for. She loved him: yes, different than the chief, but a love from years of trust and learning about each other, years of raising a child together. That was true love, not love for a moment in time.

He remembered when Hunter was five. The spirit, by then, had left Louise and was totally with the boy. They were out taking a walk holding hands. The sun was shining and Hunter was running at the edge of the river playing. Even at that age the animals loved him. He knew it was the spirit but it still was wonderful to watch. The birds would just land on his shoulders and the deer in the woods would just come up to him and let him pet them. Even though the spirit had left Louise, the animals, still treated her same. At those times he did feel like an outsider but at the same time the wonderment of what was unfolding around him kept him happy to be at least there even if on the outside looking in.

They were crossing the river on some small stones. The river was not very strong or deep here. As Louise stepped on one stone she slipped and he caught her in his arms and their faces touched. They were face to face, about an inch from each other's lips. He could hear her breath and then kissed her. To his great joy she kissed back. He could feel the tingling down to his toes. She smiled at him with that wonderful smile and about that time Hunter splashed them and ran across the river. He knew this was the beginning of their love. He could hardly wait until he could hold her and feel her softness next to him. He had waited for this a long time and now he was a little frightened. He wanted her because she loved him not because she was grateful to him. He would not worry about it now. For now, walking, holding her hand and watching Hunter was a greater feeling then he had ever known. Time would tell.

Time did tell and he and Louise became really husband and wife. When she came to him that night, he could hardly control all his feelings. The room was lighted by candle light and as she came close to him, he could see her face in the light. She loved him, it was written on her face; maybe not a great passion, but a great love. When she came into his arms and he could feel her heart beat with his, it felt like time stood still and the moment was like the earth had stood still and he could hardly breathe. They were two people frozen in time. He never forgot that moment and even here on his death bed he could still feel the love she had given him.

When he arrived at the cabin he was wondering if he was in a dream, the cabin was just as they had left it. Someone had changed the blankets and cleaned but it was almost like a shrine. He went back in his mind when he had first come here and remembered seeing her the first time. His dad had told him of the prophecy but he really didn't believe him. People made up stories when they needed something to believe in and the Indians needed that now just to keep going. More and more White men were coming into their land and they knew soon they would lose. He still could remember seeing her for the first time. Looking into the cabin and seeing the Wolf lying beside her and the Bear guarding the front door. He realized that this was something special that he had walked into. Maybe the prophecy was true. Seeing all this made him not too sure of his own disbelief.

He loved her from that moment on and it was the hardest thing he ever did to leave her in the cabin and go with his father to the governor. They both were sure they could not take her from there at

LOUISE

that time. The Indians were still all around the cabin and the drums were very loud. The fact they were still alive was even hard to believe. She was being held for some reason and at the time they didn't realize it was to have Hunter.

How does a person love someone so much as that little boy? Maybe he wasn't of his blood but he was his father. From the moment he was born he loved him. He knew at first it was because he was part of Louise but he wanted to take on the job of being his father. The person who gives the time and beliefs to a child and protect, and teaches him is their parent not the person who gave their seed. He was Hunter's father and he loved him. He was sitting by his bed and holding his other hand. The two people in life he loved so much were, as he was dying, with him. He was happy.

His mind took him back to the cabin. At the cabin he had met Hunter's father the chief.

After he had been in the cabin for a while, he saw a shadow at the door and when he turned, he saw him. He was looking all around. Bill knew he was looking for Louise and was sure this was not going to be a friendly conversation. He was a very muscular man, with long dark hair and deep eyes that almost looked black. He himself was athletic but not as tall or muscular. He wasn't afraid but wondered how to tell him why he had come. He was a lawyer for many years and hadn't returned to being a scout, so he would not be any match for this man. This man had lived in the wild and from, what Louise told him of their love, he probably would have wanted her back and not to go to another man. He had become soft with city living. He didn't want to leave Louise and Hunter for one moment. How do you tell a man you have had his woman and child for 21 years? This wasn't going to be easy.

Then the chief talked in English. Not perfect English but understandable. He told Bill he knew he was taking care of Louise and Hunter. How did he know his name? That even though he wanted her with him he appreciated Bill taking care of her and his son. He knew he had come to talk peace but the prophecy said the boy would come and he had to wait for him. He told him that he had tried to make peace for years but the White man keep pushing them out of their land and war was coming and he had no way of stopping it. He told him after loving Louise he had not hunted or killed a White person since. He said that peace would only come when people, no matter what color, could live side by side with their differences. He didn't know if that could happen.

They were so different in ways but in some ways the same. Both wanted to protect their loved ones and to keep them from harm. He wanted it the way it was when he was a boy; to run after the deer and sleep under the stars to know what was expected of you and where your life would lead you. He had thought he would have many children and a good wife, but those days were long gone. His child was a stranger to him and the woman he loved was gone. He didn't get to share all his dreams and plans for them. He didn't get to raise his son to be like him. They must be able to get along with the Whites or they would lose more than their land. He didn't understand why they ruined the land and killed animals for fun. He was sure he would never understand.

He wondered if Louise had told Bill about their love or if he thought he had hurt her. He could hardly think of how he would feel if he thought this man had hurt her. The spirit had visited him at different times in dreams. He told him how she was and about his son. He told him about this man taking care of them and that he should not worry about their welfare. He told him that the boy would come to him and together they would bring peace. He didn't know how to do that but he did believe in the spirit. If he said it would be so then it would. He wondered if he would see Louise again. Would she still love him or be afraid? Would she want to be with him or stay in the life she had? He didn't ask the spirit; he was afraid to know.

He must get this man out of here safe. This would prove to be a great task. Yes, all his tribe would help but so many had gone away from the spirit's ways and were after only their own pleasures. These groups were growing in number and strength. Soon he would not be able to hold them back. The leader was an evil man who bred hate and loved no one. This man must be stopped and that would be his task. He hoped he had the strength and the God of all with him.

It seemed to Bill that the chief was in deep thought but then he said we must go. This place is not safe for you and you need to return and take care of Louise and Hunter. So, he wasn't to bring the beginning of peace to the land, Hunter was. He didn't want the boy here. He was not an Indian; he was his son and wouldn't know how to take care of himself. He wondered if he had raised him wrong in not teaching him to be part of his heritage. What would happen if he came here? Would he know what to do to stay alive? He decided Hunter would not come back here alone. If they were to come, he would be with the boy. He still could protect him and he was sure the chief would also. Between the two of them he hoped Hunter would survive.

He didn't remember much after that only many Indians leading him to safety. He almost made it home but his horse saw a snake and bucked him off and broke his leg. He was somewhat confused and couldn't remember how long ago that had been. The pain was bad and the doctor said there was infection. He knew this was to be his last ride. But with Louise and Hunter by his side he could face anything.

Remembering

Louise held Bill's hand and tears fell from her eyes. They were tears of sadness and of great grief. She knew he was dying and they couldn't help him. She had fallen in love with him in a soft gentle way long before the spirit left her; he was kind, loving and cared about the boy. As he held Hunter as a small child, she could see the great love he had for him. She could almost see him holding the baby and kissing his chubby checks. He would show everyone the child with such pride. You would have never known he wasn't the father because he was. He wanted the boy and loved him. She remembered him taking them on walks and teaching him to ride. When Hunter was a baby, he would get up at night and carry him to her to feed and stay with them all night, and hold and rock the baby and just hold Hunter and her close. She could feel her respect turning into love maybe not like the one she had for the spirit but still a good deep love. A love that would last through all time and places; yes, she loved him.

He was trying to work with the army and help with the peace talks. He told her he felt they were just like them, he wanted peace and she knew that it was because of the boy. His father was a great chief but he was also Bill's son and it makes a difference when you love the enemy.

He never pushed her for his right as a husband. He would hold her at night and would just kiss her check. She could see the love in his eyes and knew his desires and because he loved her, he kept his distance. This started her love for him. When someone puts your feeling above their desires you know how important you are to them. You understand the love they have for you and then you begin to love them back. Her love grew and grew through the years. He was their body and soul. He made her laugh and feel safe with how she felt about the spirit and the chief. She told him about them and he seemed glad that they were good to her. She had lived over half her life with him and thought they would be together and grow old side by side. Her first love was taken away from her and now this love. After they were married, the spirit kept coming to her at night. Not as a lover but as a friend. He would let her know about the chief and his life and let her know he would visit the chief. He had told her the baby's name was to be Hunter, for he was to hunt for peace between both his kinds. Some nights in her dreams they would walk together by a beautiful stream. She never saw him as a person but as a presence. He just was there. She never talked about this to anyone, they would think her mad and sometimes she wondered if she was. That changed when Hunter told her the spirit visited him also. At least she wasn't mad and all that had happened wasn't a dream. It happened all of it, and she was so happy to know it. She could at times see the spirit in the boy's eyes and she knew he would protect him.

When she first became a wife to Bill, she remembered the great feeling of being loved. When he touched her his hands were ever so gentle. She did try not to compare what she felt with the chief but she couldn't help know they were different. This was a different type of love. Not a bad one just different. This love was quiet and sweet. This love was to seal a lifetime together. The passion in this love was different but at the same time wonderful. Neither love was just physical, both were mental. One could take a person's body but to be in union with their mind was great love. To feel the person's love for you and have them feel your love for them made the physical part just better. This man had saved her from a life of mental suffering and gave her a life of great pride and joy and he was to be honored. He had come into her life in a cabin in the woods so long ago and stayed with her and raised her baby as his own. There would never be enough ways to thank him and yet she knew she didn't have too. He loved her and that was all he wanted, just to love her.

    He had gone back to the cabin to find the chief. He told her what he was trying to do. The spirit had told her this would come to be but she didn't want him to go. She was nervous about them meeting. Why? She didn't know. They were two separate parts of her life and she would like to keep it that way. She didn't want the memories of the chief to change. She knew the spirit was with the chief when they were together so without the spirit would he still care for her? She didn't think she could take him not loving her as she stilled loved him. And would he understand the love she had for Bill and understand letting him raise their son in the white world? In the end she realized there was nothing she could do about it. Most of her life was like that. She was glad for the path it took but knew if she had her young dreams come true life would have been different. She would have missed a lot: but if you had never known it would you miss it? She wanted her memories and she was glad for her life and her great loves. He smiled at her and she smiled back. She could still see the love he had for her through all the pain. She had been so lucky to have been his wife and she didn't want to let him go.

Hunter

This was the only father he knew. This man had taken care of him all his life. He knew he wasn't his real father by seed but he was his father in every other way. He loved him and felt his mother's pain. He could see his mother holding Bill's hand with her eyes full of tears, life pouring out of her with each drop. It was very hard to see. You want to stop the pain but can't and feel even sadder because you can't.

The spirit came to him when he was about 5 years old. It was just a feeling that someone or thing was different in your mind. It talked to him and told him about his real father the chief. At first, he was afraid he was going mad but when he talked to his mother about it, she understood and told him the story about the train ride and how it had changed her life. The spirit told him of the prophecy and it took a lot of years before he understood it. He was to go back and see his father. Why did his step-father have to go back? If he had stayed home maybe this wouldn't have happened. In his heart he knew he was hoping that if Bill went back, he wouldn't need to go. But the spirit had told him, and Bill it was him. He didn't know his father except what the spirit had, told him. His dad is the man lying dying on this bed. This man taught him respect came from within and that justice and truth was the way to live your life. His dad loved his mother and kept them safe and happy all these years. This was a great man's hand he was holding. He learned about love just watching how he treated his mother. How gentleness and sweetness was not a sign of weakness but of strength. He had answered so many whys. He had picked him up and made all his hurt go away. He had made him feel like a good person with a great mind. He had given him respect for himself and had made his mother smile. His dad told him once that if he could just remember all people are the same. You can walk down the street and see people and just think in your mind about yourself or realize all these people had problems and troubles just like you and you were not the only person in the world but a small piece of mankind. If you realized that, you would give of yourself and that would be the start of peace for all kinds of people, even Indians. You would help to make the world a better place.

His real father: how does a person meet someone who gave you your life, and not know anything about them? The spirit told him about his father, but to know someone you must spend time with them and then make up your own mind of what kind of person they were. To do that, he needed to spend time with him. He would go out west on the train and, like his mother, go to the cabin and wait for his father and hopefully they would be able to start some peace talks. That is what the spirit had told him he was to do but for now he wanted to be here with his dad.

The Spirit

He had spent 21 years giving Hunter all the knowledge he needed to start the peace talks. The boy was a quick learner and had his mother's heart. He would be sad when it was time for him to go but in seeing and understanding the boy's feelings, especially with his dad dying, he knew he was the right one. He would return to the chief one more time and let him know about the boy coming and then he would go back to his rest and with him the memories of Louise and all her love and beauty. This was something he had never known in real life. He was grateful to the God of all for allowing him to have experience this. He also was grateful for the boy. He was like his own child and going through his growing up was exciting and a learning process for him. Times had changed and the problems had different names but the same lessons.

Soon Bill would have no more pain. He would join the spirit world and be at peace. He had been the perfect husband and stepfather. He had worked 21 years for their happiness and didn't ever feel like it should be any other way. He waited for Louise's love and didn't seem to mind. He was a man of great kindness and tenderness and yet could fight for justice. He had given that to Hunter. Hunter was the chief's seed but Bill had given him the knowledge to accomplish his task. To feel Louise's sadness was very hard for him.

He loved her and, like Hunter, wished he could make it better but also knew one must grieve the lost or they would never go on with their life. He watched while the silence in the room was deafening. You could hear the clock ticking on the wall. Bill was telling Louise thank you for a wonderful life and telling his son how much he loved him. He remembered when he first saw him come to the cabin. He knew then he was falling in love with her and part of him was jealous. But he also knew this was the answer to who would take care of Louise when the chief was sent away. Many times, he wanted to enter Bill and be with Louise but he knew that was wrong. She needed to find some kind of real life. He did visit her in her dreams and they talked. She was like fresh rain on your face or sweet snow falling in the woods. She made him wish to never leave her but he knew, just like the chief, he would lose her in the end. He would go back to his place and she would go on with life. Her father and mother would help her and, of course, Hunter. He would be by her side as much as he could. He knew she would understand he had to go to his father but he also knew she would fear for him.

    He would tell her in a dream he would be with the boy. He would be at first, but then Hunter would be on his own. He knew between Bill and him the boy would do well.

Sorrow

The night was coming. You could see the shadows outside, the sun going down and a great man going to his maker.

Bill died that night. They stopped the clocks, closed his eyes and cried. They had lost a great part of their life. The memories would always be with them but they would miss the man. Hunter held his mother and the spirit held her too. Hunter and His mother felt an emptiness that they knew would not be filled. The spirit knew he was going to a better place. He felt for their sadness but joy for where Bill was going.

Louise's father took care of all the arrangements, military funeral and all. Louise sat with Hunter and they talked about the 21 years of Bill. They talked about fun stuff they all did and laughed and then cried. They told each other what the man meant to them. He had played different rolls with both. He was a good and strong father and a sensitive and caring husband.

Louise's father wanted her to talk Hunter out of going to see his father. He knew after all this settled down the boy would want to go. He knew the spirit was still part of him and sometimes he wanted to yell at him to leave his family alone. First, they used his daughter and now they wanted his grandson. Bill had never been a step-son, he was his son. He became very close to him, not only had he helped with his daughter but he loved her and waited for her to love him. Most men would have been angry and would have given up let alone raise someone else's child. He knew Bill loved the boy as his own. He had tried to talk Bill out of going to the cabin. He told him that he had given more than most people and he should enjoy his family and let someone else work for the peace talks, but Bill told him until peace came no one had done enough.

He knew that because Hunter's father was Indian, Bill wanted peace even more. He wanted this for Hunter and Louise. He had told him he wondered if he met Hunter's father how he would feel and how Hunter's father would feel. He hoped they could talk and from what Bill had told him when he came back, they had talked. The chief told him his son must come. That was why he was born and why the chief had to give up Louise and Hunter. He told him the chief was grateful for him taking care of his family. This was Bill's family and he wished he had told him that but, as Bill said, it would only have caused bad feelings and Bill knew in his heart the chief had been 21 years' worth of sorrow and loss. He could never have been happy without Louise and Hunter.

When he had sent Bill out to find his daughter, he had no idea what a great man he was. At that time could think of nothing but finding his daughter and maybe, he hoped, alive. Bill helped him save her in all ways even from having the chief's baby. Even her mother didn't know that Hunter wasn't Bill's son. Her life would have been much harder; not that she would have changed it, but seeing people feeling sorry for you and looking at your son like he was a mistake would have torn her heart apart. No, Bill had made her life full of good blessings and Louise's father really was going to miss him. Maybe if he talked to the boy, he could get him not to go back and find his father. Maybe he would stay for his mother. No, he would do what he felt was best for the others. He would want to be part of finding a way to have peace. He was Bill's boy in all ways. If he went back, he would go with him and meet this chief. After all, he was his son's grandfather.

The Return

Hunter had made plans to return to the cabin. He knew the chief would watch for him there; the spirit told him. He had talked to his mother and grandfather about where it was. His mother talked about it in a very low, soft voice. Almost as if she talked too loudly the memories would go away. He knew she had held this in her heart for a very long time. She was smiling as she remembered his father, a sweet smile like when you see a baby smile. She had loved his father he could tell. She was so young to have so much happen to her but it didn't seem to have made her bitter on life, it seemed to make her love life more. She had told him more then once that he was the greatest blessing she had and she was so happy to have been able to bring him into the world. He was a gift and she never stopped thanking the Lord for him. Just thinking about this made him feel very much loved and very lucky to have such a mother. He didn't think she would remarry because he knew she loved Bill with a very deep love and he was sure she loved his father but how he wasn't sure. Maybe he would ask the chief about their love if the time was right.

First, he needed to get to his father and they needed to make a plan of how to start this idea of peace. It wouldn't be easy. First, he was presuming his father still wanted this after all that had happened. Maybe he hated the White man even more. He was presuming he would even get there. There were so many angry things that had been done to these people over the last 21 years; he wondered if there ever could be a common ground for understanding that would lead to some kind of side-by-side living. He knew that all the Indians would know who he was. After all, he was the son of a chief. After he said that he stopped and wondered how a person acted as a son of a chief. Yes, the spirit taught him all the ways of the Indian but hearing it and living it were two different things. Did he go back as a White or an Indian? Wearing a head dress and a suit would not do. They would have to sit and talk and open up to what each needed to start the first step of getting along. One little step would start the whole thing but finding out what that little step was would be the thing that would take the time. And also, there were those on both sides that didn't want them to get along. What of those? They would continue to try to ruin anything mending all the years of hurt. Some would do it for greed, some for vengeance, some because that was all they were taught. It would take both sides to realize that there were more people that wanted to get along then the ones who wanted war.

He knew the spirit would tell his father he was coming so he should be able to get to the cabin alive, after that he was on his own. How did he address the chief, Father, Chief? Would they understand each other or had the years hardened his heart? There was no point about worrying about these things because he needed to do whatever it took. It was his job from the day he was born. His mother had no fear of him going to the cabin and he was sure it was because she had been close to his father. And when a person shares that kind of closeness, they seem to understand what the person is capable of. He knew she loved his step father very much but he also knew she was in love with the chief, his father.

He had heard that, after being with his mother, the chief worked for a way to stop all the hate. His tribe, believing in the prophecy, also believes in his son. That was him and he hoped he could be worthy of it. He would go see all the right people in the government to get their approval in his quest. If he didn't have their approval, his trip would be in vain. He could not make promises he couldn't give. Part of him knew that the peace would be one-sided and the Whites would still make it hard for the Indian, but at least some would survive and be able to live together and the killing and hate could start to end.

He would go to Washington and get the approval to travel west and have peace talks. Most of the people there already knew him because of his step-father and he had followed in his foot steps and studies to become a lawyer. He had studied all about the Indian problem, as they called it. Most had heard of the stories of his mother and the prophecy, but they didn't believe it. They were just sure he was a smart young man who was a great speaker and maybe could talk to these savages. He was part savage and they didn't even have a clue. It would have made a difference to them if they had known. They would see the Indian in him and not see him for who he was. That is why he never told anyone who his father was and why his mother had to hold all her memories in her heart.

He loved his mother. She had always told him the truth and had made him know the power of love. The spirit had taught him the way but his mother taught him the how. He knew his grandfather wanted to go but he felt that it was to be him alone, not an army of people.

He had stayed in town for a few days getting everything ready. Some army troops were going with him even though he didn't want them too. He really thought it would be better if he went alone. He would have to deal with them when the time came to let him go on alone.

The train would take them and their horses to the small town near the cabin, twenty-one years ago it was just the end of the tracks and just forest; now, it was a stop for the train, on its way out west. The cabin was a good ten miles in the forest and the ground around the town had been left alone to still be like nature made it. This had been done because of his grandfather. The land around the cabin and burial ground was to be a natural forest. No one was to enter. This had kept some peace but still there were the poachers and men that wanted to get the Indian relics. It seemed all that tried were found dead. After a while people were afraid of the forest and stayed out. He now was going to go in. He hoped his father would be there and help, but only time would tell.

But now he needed to get home and gather all his equipment for the trip and talk to his mother and ask if she wanted him to give the chief a message.

Going Home

She sat on the train and she was going home after twenty-one years. No one knew yet that she had left. They would have tried to stop her. She would have never left Bill for he had taken care of her and Hunter and she loved him; but when Bill died she felt she had the right to find her great love. She loved in different ways. Bill was the stable life, what most women are lucky to find: friendship, caring, honest love. But the chief was first love, sweet love, crazy love the kind most people never have. She had this at 19 and then it was taken away. She knew it was what had to happen and she had to leave it. It was her destiny. But maybe now she could at least just live in the cabin and remember. The memories would last a life time.

She wondered if the chief even thought of her and if he had married and had other children and if he would love Hunter. She knew the spirit would have told him about Hunter and that he would know about Bill. But she also knew he would understand because of the prophecy that his son, Hunter must be raised as White.

She had tried not to remember for 21 years because when the memories would creep into her dreams she longed to go back. She would feel badly because Bill lay beside her and she loved him, but wished she could have been with another. A person could love more then one, both deeply and both different. Bill understood that, they had talked about what had happened in the cabin and she told him how wonderful it was. If he was jealous, he didn't show it. He seemed to understand the difference and I think Bill thought he got the best one. He had her and grown up with her and the two of them became friends and then lovers. He raised Hunter as his own and did a wonderful job of it. Hunter knew of the chief but loved Bill as his dad.

She had told her mother and father she was going shopping when she left the house. She didn't take anything extra with her when she went to the train station; she got a ticket on the train and acted like it was for a fun ride. She tried to wear her best dress for the trip and hoped she would be able to find the cabin. The place where she had gotten off the train twenty-one years ago now had a small city near the tracks. She had taken money to buy the things she needed. Even though the spirit lived in Hunter she still had all the skills he had taught her. She would buy a horse and go to the cabin. Bill had told her the cabin was still there and even had shown her on a map. She thought he knew she would go back. Funny, how things are sometimes just meant to be.

She could hear the train rolling down the track. She had no fear of harm but more fear of not finding what she was looking for. Did she think the chief would come to her? No, he had a mission to fill also; no, she was looking for the peace in her heart. She wanted the peace, she felt in that cabin twenty-one years ago. The simple feeling of belonging where you were and knowing who you are. That peace might be gone but she had to try. She needed to know. Maybe the animals would still trust her and that she hoped for. They brought peace in themselves. Just the ones with nature were a great joy. She knew Indians believe in the prophecy and would not harm her for fear of the spirit. She hoped the spirit would join her again but, in her heart, she knew he would stay with Hunter until the prophecy was fulfilled and then go back to his resting place and leave them forever. He would be just one of their wonderful memories.

LOUISE

She had left a note for her dad and he would know where she had gone. He would worry but also knew nothing would happen to her. He would send Hunter and that was supposed to happen. So, he would think the spirit made her go. Hunter would come soon but she hoped she would have a few days alone in the cabin to just remember the great love she had shared there. Would she go back to her mother and father, she didn't know. That would be something that would depend on a lot of possibilities. She had to consider her son and her family also, she didn't want them to worry or be sad. She would not worry about that now. She just wanted to get to the cabin. Bill had told her it was just like she had left it. She would just go in and lay down on the bed and sleep and dream and remember.

When she got off the train she looked around. When she had been here twenty-one years ago there was just forest and now people, houses, stores, livestock and even a trading post. She stood out in the crowd because of her clothes and hair and the very fair skin. When a person lived out here the sun took a toll on the skin. She went right to the general store and bought a simple dress and hat worn by all the women in this town. She asked if she could store her other clothing somewhere, not because she wanted them but to make the people feel she was just out for a change. She lied and said her husband would be on the next train and they were out for a little adventure. She came ahead to get rooms and see what they needed. They seemed to believe her, so when she asked where she could buy horses, they didn't think anything about it.

When she got to the stable, she saw the most wonderful black stallion ever. She smiled and wondered if she had met his father long ago. She road him back to the train. The men at the stable didn't want her to go near him because he was wild and no one had been able to tame him; but as she walked to him his head bowed down and rested against hers. Her whole body shivered and her heart beat faster and faster and her mind kept saying; you are home, you are home at last. She turned looking into stunned eyes and said ever so softly I will take him please. She asked for a saddle also, even though she didn't need one but these men had seen enough. She also bought another pack horse and went back to the general store and stocked up on some staples, telling the store keeper she and her husband were going riding when he got there. The store keeper told her it was safe in the forest but not to go near the burial ground.

In her mind she laughed. Someone should have told her that twenty-one years ago. But then she wouldn't have had the great advantage and love she had found and the greatest part of her life, Hunter. She smiled at him and told him thanks for all the help and left. She went to the stable and the stallion was saddled and the pack horse ready. The stable man went to help her get on but before he got near her, she was on the back of the horse and riding off. He just looked in utter amazement. He had heard stories about a White woman who seemed to be able to charm animals and he wondered if he had just met her.

She sat on the horse and felt the warm sun in her face and the wind in her hair. She felt free. The horse picked up its pace and the wind grew stronger and her eyes let the little water drops of tears of joy run down her checks. She was going home to the place she had walked in for a short while and lived in her dreams all these years. She thought she might burst with joy and then she saw them, at the entrance of the forest, Indians. They were the bad Indians trying to keep the hate alive. All of a sudden, the spirit entered her. The horse stated to run full out to the burial ground. She could hear the screams as they came after her, but she had no fear for it had been a long time since she had been one with the spirit and the joy was greater than the fear.

When they reach the burial ground the horse entered without stepping on one relic. The pack horse had galloped into the forest. The horse turned, and she saw the Indians at the entrance with fear in their eyes. You could tell they now knew who she was. Even though they were feeless warriors, they were afraid of the dead and of spirits. The leader looked into her eyes and you could see the hate and yet the wonderment. The great horse, the White woman, and the spirit in the burial ground. He put down his knife and told the rest to be quiet. The trees let the wind sway them and seemed to tell the story. He had seen the prophecy right in front of him; now he had to pick what side he would follow. For this young warrior it would be a hard task. They turned and left.

Louise got off the horse and lay down and the spirit put her into a deep sleep. She would rest with his ancestors and be kept safe until he could bring help.

The chief's tribe guarded the cabin. They waited for the son of the chief to come back. They had heard the woman was here and had been saved by the spirit in the burial ground. She slept and their tribe surrounded the burial ground and protected her. Her son would come for her and meet his father. The drums were telling of the woman's return and all the tribes could hear them. It was time for peace talks; soon her son would be here, the son of a great chief who could lead them to peace.

Hope

Stillness fell over the forest. All that could be heard was the sound of one-horse walking. Then there stood a figure in the mist. He wore a headdress that fell to the ground and his hair was black as night, his body solid and muscular, his skin was brown like copper. His face held no expression but his insides screamed.

    The circle of Indians opened and let him pass. She was ten feet from him, he could see her face. He remembered the soft touch of her skin and her silk hair on his face. He felt like air would not fill his lungs. He was a great chief and he could feel his eyes fill with longing to see her closer and he could feel his arms ache to hold her and just to hear her speak and smile. Yes, smile at him. She slept the deep sleep of one in a trance. He knew the spirit had done this. His son was coming at last and the boy's mother was sleeping waiting for him. He must not touch her. He would have to wait until the spirit let him go to her. He turned his horse around and the circle closed around her and he didn't look back. He was a chief and his eyes were full of tears. No one could see this. His tears were years of yeaning and worry. Tears of sorrow of twenty-one years lost and tears of joy for seeing her again. His inside shook he wanted her so badly, but he had to wait. Maybe she would have forgotten him, that was this greatest fear. Not to have her remember their love. He still had the cave in the mountains ready for her. He always wished she would come back to him. If he could this time, he would take her with him and they could start all over. Maybe the spirit would be kind and give him and her rest. The day she was taken from here was something he dreamed of every night. He would wake with great sorrow. He would reach beside and want to find her but she was gone, the spirit had told him about his son and Bill. He was glad he was a gentle man and a good step-father for Hunter. He knew this was what had to happen and he knew Louise did what the spirit told her. Her love for Bill he was sure was need. But the love for him was lasting in his heart. He knew this but, in his mind, he worried that the spirit would take the memories away and she would not remember. He did care much about peace with the White men; he loved his people but he wanted some time in his life to have a little peace of his own. He wanted to sleep beside the woman he loved and not dream of her leaving. He wanted to wake to her smile and kiss. He had taken a path up the mountain for his eyes were showing his entire feelings. The tears dropped onto his horses back and he could feel the warmth of them on his check. He couldn't let his people see this but he needed to have some time to come to the knowledge that maybe the wait was over and just that was almost too much to believe. He had for twenty-one years waited. He did all the spirit had asked of him and more. This woman had given him a heart he would have never known. He had been in battles and been hurt more then once and never a tear or fear but this woman, so close, opened his heart until it hurt with fear of losing her again. It took all his strength to keep going away from her. He wanted to just go and take her with him and let His people and her people work out their differences because she and he had no differences; they had a son.

When his son came, they would have to spend time in the cleansing tent. They would learn from each other through the spirit. He would gain the entire chief's knowledge and he would know his entire son's. This would set the chief free to go to Hunter's mother for Hunter was the one to bring the peace.

He went to the cave he had made for them twenty-one years ago. He came here often; he kept it all ready for her to come home. It was a good home. The cave was large with room for storage of food and wood and would keep them warm in the winter. He had kept the bedding and clothing new each year. He would sit by the fire and remember. Sometimes he could smell her skin like she was sitting beside him. When he looked at the stars, he could see her eyes sparkling back at him and when he felt the wind on his face, he could feel her lips touch his. This was what made him go on, the thought that he would see her again and, today, he had. She was still the most beautiful woman he had ever seen. Yes, she had aged as he had, but her beauty was from within. You could see it in her eyes and he wanted to look into her eyes and see that she still loved him. He remembered when he first saw her that he was going to kill her and now the White woman was all he wanted for the rest of his life. He heard the wolves howling. They knew she was back. No one had seen a white wolf since she left and he knew that one was coming to greet her. He got up and mounted his horse to return to his tribe. He would have to be there when the boy came and they would have to make the cleansing tent ready. So, for now, he once again must put his wants and great needs aside and hoped that soon he would be able to be with the one he loved.

The Return

Hunter felt the spirit leave. He was on his way to talk to his mother and tell her it was time for him to go to his father. He stopped: the spirit had left him, but before when this had happened, he was left with a feeling of peace. This time there was a sense of urgency. His mother had gone back by herself. He must clear his mind and think of the right plan. He would not wait for the army. He would go home and get his gear and take the train and find his mother. She had spent most of her life doing what others wanted so he could not be angry she did something for herself. She was going to his father. He didn't know his father so he had great fear for her. What if he didn't remember her? Maybe the spirit had taken the memory away. What if he hurt her? Then the prophecy was all a lie because he would not bring peace no matter how much he knew he should. He would bring sorrow and anger. But, then, she would not want that. He would have to think of all she gave up for peace. He couldn't let that be in vain and he knew the spirit loved her so she must be alright. He would start thinking positive.

When he reached the house, his grandfather was there. You could see the worry on his face. He must not let him know he, too, was worried. His grandfather ran down the stairs and asked if she had gone back? He knew the spirit would tell Hunter what was happening. But all Hunter really knew was that she was alright; and then the spirit returned.

He told his grandfather she was sleeping in the burial ground and was protected by his father's tribe. She was in a trance and was at perfect peace. The chief had come but did not enter the burial ground. He had left and gone to the mountains to reflect on his life with her. The spirit told him his father waited for him to come. He didn't want to tell his grandfather Louise didn't want to come back.

He told his grandfather that the two of them should get on the train and go to her. He and his grandfather would start the peace talks and not the army that was getting ready to go. The plan would be to get his father's tribe to start the peace talks with others. But first they needed to get his mother to the cabin and he had to go to the cleansing tent with his father. Hunter said that while he was with his father, his grandfather could take care of Louise. His mother had a right to have a choice where to spend the rest of her life. Her young life was taken, but now all her responsibilities were met and she could choose her own path. Hunter could feel the spirit's strong emotions on this. The spirit had taken her life and he wanted to give some of it back.

When Louise's father and Hunter went home to pack, they were afraid to tell her mother that she had gone back to the cabin, but her mother seemed to already know. She and Louise had talked about the cabin and her mother understood she loved Hunter's father. Louise never thought she could go back because she believed in her commitment to Bill. Things had changed with Bill's death. Louise's mother told the two to sit for they must know the story before going after her.

When Louise came back to the train, she looked at peace. I could tell, as a mother, she had become a woman. We did not talk about it for about two days and then I asked her to tell me of her adventure. I remember she smiled and took my hand and told me of the spirit and the chief. You could see the spirit in her eyes and could tell just by looking he also loved her. They both wanted me to know she was not hurt but deeply loved and loved deeply back. She knew she was with child and that the baby was a boy and would be called Hunter. She had wanted to stay with the chief but the spirit had told her of the path she must take. Her fear was when the spirit left her, and went to Hunter, she would feel the emptiness and the loss even more then she did now. I looked at my daughter and saw a strong woman soon to be a mother and a person who would put her wants aside for others. This made me proud. Their love was one not many people find. Most of us love and share with each other, but their love was being part of each other in every way, two different worlds, two different lives and one great love for each other. And that love was so great they gave each other up. So, you see she has gone home where she left her heart and mind twenty-one years ago. They must not try to take her back. She must see the chief and then make up her mind. She had a right for a least that.

    She loved her daughter and wanted her with her but wanted her to be happy and that could be never seeing her again. Hunter would be part of both lives and wouldn't have to give her up but maybe they did. She couldn't imagine the spirit would let anyone hurt her but if the chief didn't remember their time together then she would need her mother and father. That would be an arrow in one's heart. The memories and dreams of the past would all be lost and Louise would be very empty. So, they must go slow and make sure they didn't rush her or make her mind up for her. Give the child time and peace. Give her time to see if that moment in time was real and still there. Her mother rose from her chair and left them in silence.

    Hunter knew what had happened to his mother but he really never felt the full emotions of it until know. The spirit with him made him feel that it was a wonderful time for her but the spirit left out the loss. He left out the wanting and dreaming and remembering and hoping. He left out making a promise to Bill and giving up her hopes. How much did his mother's heart hurt? If it was in his power, he would help her be where she wanted to be no matter what the spirit wanted. The spirit told him he too, wanted her happy even if it was with someone else.

    His father and he left for the train. The spirit told him his mother was alright and not to worry. Silly not to worry because he was going into a culture and a family he never met. He would meet the great chief, his father, and then what? The cleansing tent, and he had no idea what that would be like. Let's hope all the spirit had taught him over the years would be enough.

Sorting one's Thoughts

He could hear the drum from his cave. The boy and his grandfather were coming; they would go to the burial ground. The drums told of a White wolf sleeping beside her and a Bear at the entrance. The spirit could enter the sacred ground and because he was in the boy, Hunter could go and get his mother. They would take her to the cabin. Their cabin where the spirit would give them back their lives. She had come back on her own and his mind kept telling him she would only come if she remembered and still loved him and he smiled, but then the other part of his mind wondered if the spirit made her come and he could feel the uncertainness of the joy. He couldn't sleep. Every time he closed his eyes, he saw her lying beside him and to awaken and not have her there was almost too much to bear.

He rose, mounted his horse and started the ride back to reality. He was a chief and he would do all the responsibilities that title came with. He set Louise deep in his heart in the place he had kept her for twenty-one years and rode off to the cleansing tent. The elders would be waiting for him and the boy. They would learn from each other through the spirit. He wondered if the boy looked like him or had his mother's beautiful brown eyes. Maybe the boy would be angry at what happened to his mother, if he really knew what happened he would only be sad that they were parted. No, his son would be strong in mind and body. He was the son of a chief and he would lead his people to peace. He knew that it would take generations to undo the pain and hurt that was done on both sides but if the frightening and hate would stop the young would bring the peace by just not being aware of the difference. Side by side a new way would come one of tolerance and understanding. The Indians would lose the most but as long as they were told of their heritage, his ancestors and he would always be alive in them.

In the cleansing tent he would learn all about the twenty-one years Hunter was with his mother. He would see her life. He was sure he would not understand how the White lived. In his tribe the woman was for the man and to keep his life simple at home. She would cook, gather wood, and clean the animals the men hunted and have the children of the future but in Louise's life: women were treated like delicate flowers that would break. Louise was strong but he must admit he would want to keep her close. He didn't even know if he could let her out of his site to gather wood. Maybe this was how White men loved and his people had never shared the great love a man could have for a woman. He knew his father loved his mother. He could see them smile at each other when they thought no one was looking. Why does a man have to pretend that loving a woman is weak? He was finding out loving a woman was the hardest trial he had ever faced and yet held the greatest reward. He was afraid to see how she lived. Could she give that up for the life of a chief's woman? Maybe not for the way of life but for the love he would give her. Louise was a woman who took the good with the bad and made a better life for all. She had given up her wants for those of nations. She knew what mattered in life and, because of her, he did too.

In the tent the heat would put them in a dream state. They would travel through time past and present. They would become father and son. All the years apart would be taken away. The learned ones would watch and keep guard. There were still many White and Indian that didn't want peace. Louise's father would take care of her in the cabin and his tribe would also keep watch. The Wolf and Bear would not leave her. Even though the spirit was with Hunter, it had left some of its blessing with Louise. She would always be one with the animals and the forest would hold no fear or harm for her.

As he traveled on, his tribe joined with him. It was a magnificent sight. He led an army ready to die for whatever he said. He was their leader and they would follow Hunter when the time was right. They all knew of Louise and respected the mother of Hunter. She was considered different then their women. She was part spirit and that made them respect and fear her. They were a race of superstitions. The fear of the dead and the spirit world was something all tribes feared and that would help in the talks, for Hunter was with spirit and that would give him great power. All the chiefs would fear the spirit within and make their people listen.

The Young Chiefs Return

When Hunter and his grandfather got off the train, they went right to the stable to buy horses. The man there remembered Louise. He would never forget her and the black stallion. He asked the boy if maybe she had a stable that raised horses. He had never seen a woman able to ride like her. Hunter told him she had a great teacher and smiled. The man told him the pack horse had come back. They thought she had gone to the hotel and not tied up the horse properly and it wandered back to the stable. He thought she would be back for it. He still had all the provision; and the horse and told them he would get them ready for them. He felt bad that they hadn't looked for her but with the way she rode the stallion they were sure she was alright. When they figured out, she might need help they had no idea where to look. No one had seen her leave town. She had told them her husband was coming so they were waiting for him and would help him search for her. They had heard the drums and were afraid of the worst.

Hunter and his grandfather took the horses and pack horse and left telling him not to worry. They knew where she was.

When they got to the burial ground Hunter had to hold his grandfather back. You cannot enter, they will kill you. I must go; just me and the spirit. He saw her lying, sleeping, and the black horse standing beside her and of course the white Wolf. The Wolf turned and, at first, bared its teeth and then knew it was the spirit and lay back down. The drums were louder, knowing the boy chief had returned with the spirit.

    He picked up his mother and took her to her father. The horse and Wolf followed. He mounted the stallion and held his mother close. She was still in a deep sleep. The Indians surrounding the burial ground had left. He and his grandfather took Louise to the cabin. On the way they were being followed. They were sure it was the same Indians keeping watch over Louise at the burial ground. When they saw the cabin, it was just like Hunter remembered in his dreams. The fire was burning and the smell of food was in the air. They had gone ahead and prepared the place for them. This was a different kind of feeling, one of importance and one of not deserving. He knew he was the son of a chief but he hadn't even proved himself worthy. But maybe it was for his mother because he knew his father loved her very much and so did the chief's people. When they entered the cabin, he lay Louise on the bed and covered her up. He asked the spirit how long she would be in a trance and the spirit told him to let her rest, her journey was not over yet. He told his grandfather to watch over his mother because it was time he went to his father. When he left the cabin, the black stallion came up to him and he mounted it. They spirit had told him about the cleansing tent and how he would know all he needed after this ritual but part of him was worried that never really living something could really make you understand it. If he was to help with peace, he would have to try to keep the Indians from being used. He knew most Whites would always think they were just Indians and really had no rights but to him they were here first and had all the rights, just not the numbers. More and more people were settling out west and pushing them farther and farther and soon there would be no place to go. His hope was that their children would belong and learn the White way and still keep their heritage.

He seemed to know what way to ride. As he came near the camp a band of Indians surrounded him. They stayed at a distance but were escorting him to the tent. How could they think he could take his father's place? The spirit seemed to think all this was going to work out but then he was a spirit and seemed to believe everything, but right now Hunter wasn't sure. He did not fear death. He feared not being able to fulfill his part of the prophecy.

As he entered the camp, he saw who he was sure was his father. He sat on a white horse. His headdress reached the ground and Hunter could not read his expression on his face. Hunter had learned his father's language from the spirit so he greeted him. The first words from the chief were to ask if his mother was safe? Hunter told him she was at the cabin with her father and the spirit still had her in a trance that she was in a deep sleep, that she was peaceful and resting. He could see the great concern on his face. This man, his father; really loved his mother, you could see it in his face. He knew some about him through the spirit but seeing him he was sure he knew very little. He sat on the horse like it was part of him. His chest was bare and very muscular. Part of him could see himself in his face. He had no idea if he was happy to see him but that didn't matter for their lives were to become one in that tent. They both dismounted their horses and entered the tent. The time had come to have their minds become one.

Hunter changed into a loin cloth. His skin was light brown with suntan lines; he knew he looked funny. He was a lawyer and even though he spent lots of time outside he would never have the bronze skin of his father. His skin was the joining of two different shaded people. He sat across the fire from his father and they began to smoke the peace pipe. After that he felt like he was in a dream world. He walked through time in his father's world. He saw years before his father was born and understood the great peace of being one with nature. He saw the great oneness of his tribe. How they knew who and what they were and what was expected of them. He was sure his father was seeing the White man's life with all its problems caused by greed and hate and not just for different kinds of people, but for each other. He could hear the drums in the background and feel the heat and sweat on his body.

It was like seeing life on the outside, being there but not being seen. Through the years the head of the prophecy passed down from generation to generation. He knew how his father had felt when he first saw his mother at the burial ground. His father wanted to be the one the prophecy was talking about and he wanted to kill his mother and then didn't want to be without her.

He saw that his father was going to take his mother away and went to the mountains to prepare a place for them and his son. He was going to not follow the prophecy and run with her and his son. He saw how he had regretted this idea years later knowing he must do the will of the spirit and what was best for his people. And he felt the pain when his father returned from the mountains and she was gone. He felt the twenty-one years of loneliness and deep sadness his father carried. He had spent the years working for what she had to go away for and raise his son somewhere else for peace.

The chief saw the White man's life and began to understand the lack of understanding they had for the Indian. The White man had too much pressure and not time for just being alone with nature; to sit by a fire, walk in the woods; spend time with other men in the tent of learning. The work they did to keep all their passions alive gave them little time to enjoy them and even less to be with true family. He knew Hunter was taught something different, but this helped to make sense out of the White man's hate. They were wandering through time looking for what he already had - peace within. He saw their bad times in the past and how they had come to this land for freedom. He could see they also had men who hated so much they couldn't see right from wrong. The Indians had ones like this too. They both were people who didn't have the understanding of living a true life, just a life made for them. But he also saw the many that wanted to live in peace. He saw how Bill had taken care of Hunter and Louise and how he had showed him how a man should be strong and gentle. He could see Louise's warmth and love in Hunter. He could also see this would take time and he understood that it would also not be fair for the Indian but that Hunter would give all he had to make the best for both of his people. A very large task for a person and yet he felt this son of his was ready. In seeing his life, he could see his strength and honor. He might be a pale skin but he had an Indian's heart. The chief knew once they transferred knowledge, he would be free to go to Louise. He worried the years might have taken the greatness of their love and made it just a dream.

Most of his people were ready to have peace even with change. They knew, as he did, that life would never be the same; to try and fight for that was hopeless, they must learn to live with the White man and bring their ways with them. If Hunter could get them to try, they would at least begin the peace. It would be their children's children who would finally be part of the White world but at least they could help them. The heat in the tent was making him go even deeper into a trance and join with his son. They, together, could do this, he was sure.

Home

Louise awoke in the cabin. At first, she thought she was dreaming, the fire was lit and the glimmering of light took her mind back twenty-one years. She was lying on her side and could feel his body against her. But she turned and in the bed beside her was the white Wolf. Her father was sitting by the bed and held her hand. He told her that Hunter and he had taken her out of the burial ground and had taken her here. She noticed the Wolf asleep and didn't seem to mind her father being beside her. He told her Hunter had gone to his father and the cleansing tent. She longed to see him again. She wondered if he had forgotten her and she was just a dream to him. It didn't matter, she was going to stay at the cabin and live out her life. She would have the Wolf and the Bear to keep her company. She belonged here and felt at last she was home. Her son would be the new chief and would be safe and happy. Her father and mother could come see her whenever they wanted but, she was staying here in the cabin. She could ride and go to town for her supplies and the Wolf and Bear would be her protection, and she knew that she also was someone the Indians would protect. She was the mother of the new chief and the woman from the prophecy. She could hear the drums and knew Hunter and his father were in the tent and becoming one in mind. She knew her son would now know the love his father and she had shared and what they had to give up for others. He would also have to give his life to this work and she knew he would and she hoped he would be happy with it. She did not regret what had happened in these twenty-one years but she was glad she was back to the beginning here in the cabin. She smiled at her father and she slowly told him her story. He didn't tell her that her mother had told them for he wanted to know how she told it. She seemed at peace with it and he could feel the tears for her loss touch his check. She wiped them away and told him not to feel bad, for her life had been full of love and great joy. She had walked into a dream and when she came out, she was greeted by a great and good man, Bill, and now she was walking back into that dream and she felt like a warm breeze was blowing in her heart and she could let the joy of loving the chief out at last. She didn't even know his name. She just knew he was the man she deeply loved, her first love and her greatest love. No matter what happened next, she had been given a split second of life that was perfect and most people never see that. She was blessed.

She would stay in the cabin and live with nature and be one with the animals. The Spirit had given her that gift and a great gift it was. She wondered if the spirit would stay with Hunter or return to his resting place. She wished that, once more, she could feel his presence with her. The peace he brought was so pure. You felt like you were on a feather floating through the air on a warm breeze. To have shared that was unexplainable. It would be like explaining how the trees must feel when the wind blows through them, Or the sun shinning down on a stream: just great peace.

Her father seemed to understand. He rose and went to the fire and brought her some food. He told her the Indians had come with food and clothes for her. They were Indian clothes, like the ones he found her in. but these ones were decorated with many more beads and feathers, like they were the clothes of a queen. They know you're Hunter's mother and I know they will take care of you. He told her he understood why she wanted to stay and that her mother would understand also. He did smile and tell her they would bring a little more furniture because if he and her mother came there was only one chair. They both laughed. And she could see her father's eyes showed a glimmer of moisture. As he looked at her, he could see the tiny sparkles in her eyes. They were drops of love remembered. She would be happy here and they would come often to see her. He would stay until all was settled and Hunter knew and approved. He wondered how his grandson was getting along with his father and if the chief still loved his daughter or was, she just a means to an end, that end being Hunter. He hoped not, for Louise didn't remember it that way. He hoped she was seeing what really happened not what a young girl frightened would want to remember. Louise had a way of always making even bad things turn into good ones. The drums were almost singing know. They were gentle and calming, almost like a lullaby. Someone was being born or maybe being renewed. He could feel the warmth of the fire and the sound of the drums and fell asleep a very calm deep sleep. All seemed well.

The Understanding

As they came out of the tent, Hunter was wearing a head dress and his father stood beside him with his hand on his shoulder. His father was taller and much more muscular. He spoke to his people and told them Hunter was to lead them to peace, a peace with great cost. Their time was over and the peace would be for their children and their grand children. They would learn the White man ways and try to bring the goodness of their ancestors with them. They would never change the way of the White man but there was a way to bring more knowledge of nature and the Indian way to them. It would not happen over night and there would be lots on both sides trying to end the peace, but his people must be the leaders of the peace.

The great spirit of all wanted this. He knew that the spirit was with his son and he still remembered how peaceful it was when the spirit was with him. He wondered how long the spirit would stay on Earth. There would be a time the spirit would have to leave and be at rest. The spirit was many warriors of the past in one great presence. To have been part of the prophecy was more then he could have asked for. To have been able to find oneself in another was worth more than life itself. If Louise remembered and still loved him that would truly be happiness. In the tent he had learned all about her life with Bill and Hunter. He was grateful for Bill, that he took care of his woman and son so well. He could see how hard it would be to get the White man to understand the Indian. He could now understand how the hate had built over the years. It didn't take many self-serving people to make hate. It would take a lot to bring understanding after so many years of hate and hurt. They were all just people but if you would have told him that twenty-two years ago, he would have thought you were crazy. He could see his people having to change their ways and the next generation would be closer to peace but peace would take more than one generation. Hunter would start it and with the help of his God and their spirit it could come true. The drums were very loud now and the dancing had begun. This was the time of great joy. The boy chief has come to live among them and bring his help to their race. His people looked up at them coming out of the tent and gave shouts of joy. It was time to sing and dance and celebrate because the days ahead would be hard and some very sorrowful. He turned to his son and smiled and could see the spirit in his eyes. After a time, he would be able to go to the cabin and see Louise at last and maybe, just maybe, she would remember their love and return to him.

The New Chief

In the tent Hunter had learned all about his second family. He had drunk up knowledge like sweet wine. Part of him was angry for the way the Indians were treated and part of him was angry for the way the Indians treated the whites. So much hate over the years and most just caused by misunderstandings. This was a great task given to him. He had to work for peace and try to get what he could for his second family. They would have to give up the most but their children's children would get the rewards for their sacrifice. The spirit would stay with him for a while yet, to help him learn even more about life and death. He had been born for this task and no other. He would do what was expected of him and do his best to make his father proud and he knew that Bill would be watching him also and he wanted him to see that he had given his all to the task. He was unsure how to start but then, all things great have an unexpected beginning. He would stay here with his second family for a while and then return home and start through the law getting some rights for them. When you find your place in life a wonderful peace fills you up and you see all ahead as an adventure not a task. He felt like that now. He had started to do what he was born for. He had made the first steps in the tent with his father and knew he would continue on with the spirit.

His father would be free at last to live his life letting someone else carry the burden and responsibility. The great chief could go after his woman: Hunter's mother. Hunter knew she still loved him and he loved her. He wished them happiness; they had waited long enough to be together. He sat by the fire with his father and listened to the drums and watched the dance and wondered how he could have been so lucky to have been part of this.

The Reunion

Louise had wakened early and gone to the river for water. She washed and dressed in the clothes the Indians had brought her. She did not braid her hair because she remembered the chief stroking her hair with his strong gentle hands just as they went to sleep and with the slight wind blowing it felt like he was there. The Wolf was running in and out of the water like a child having fun. She couldn't believe the beauty he was of nature and just to see him was more than she could have hoped for but he even slept and ate with her. She didn't know why she deserved this but she was grateful. The Bear was always close but didn't come up to her and the Eagle flew over her cabin all day and brought her food he had caught. She was blessed and she knew it.

Her father had left about a week before, after making sure she had all the supplies he thought she needed. Her father still didn't understand that the animals and Indians would make sure of that. There were Indians camped all around the cabin. No one that shouldn't could get through would. They were there to protect and take care of her. She had protected and taken care of their boy chief. She smiled that she who had been given such a wonderful gift would be honored by the ones she felt she should thank.

She walked up to the cabin and sat on the steps. She could feel the sun on her face and there was still mist in the forest. The Wolf was sitting beside her and raised it head. She looked into the woods and saw the chief coming. She lost her breath at the sight of him and her heart was beating so hard in her chest it felt like it would burst. She felt her cheeks go red and her face turn white. He was here only ten feet way. She was afraid to move. Was this just a dream?

The mist in the forest made it look like a dream. She could still remember the feel of his skin next to hers and his strong body holding her all night. Had he come for her or was he just coming to tell her about Hunter? She had not fought her father and Bill from taking her from the cabin twenty-one years ago. Would he understand or would just the fact she left take enough away from their bond to make a small but large enough crack in their love for each other to make it unattainable. She felt faint.

He slowly rode toward her. As he came closer, she rose and could see his eyes and they were locked on her. His eyes were like looking on a lake of water. The sun showed the small amount of sparkle. Was he crying? If so, was it joy or sorrow? Her eyes were very much crying. The drops fell down her cheeks and she could taste the salt; her hands were folded at her waist and the tears hit them. When he was about two feet away, he calmly dismounted his horse.

They both were older but he still was a strong and graceful man. He walked up to her and put his hand on her cheek and touched her lips like a feather. She was breathing so hard she felt she would faint and as she swayed, he held her close. She felt his body against her and she told him very softly 'I love you and have since the day I met you.' His whole body shivered and he bent down and kissed her as if it was the first and last kiss they would ever have. He loved her too. This was their time at last. They walked into the cabin and closed the door. The wolf sat outside in front of the door and the bear came close enough to keep every one away. The drums started telling the story of the lovers reunited and the father and mother of the great chief Hunter had finally been able to be together.

This story could be about many people who through the years gave up their happiness for others. People who knew what giving was all about. Not all had happy endings but all did great works even if there were not drums to tell their story.

Hunter spent his life trying to help bring peace and Louise and the Chief grew old together. This story doesn't end. It is the beginning with a new life for Hunter, and a happy ending for Louise.

CPSIA information can be obtained
at www.ICGtesting.com
Printed in the USA
BVHW080235220522
637693BV00001B/69